1997

BEAR AND
HIS DAUGHTER

➤

S T O R I E S

Books by Robert Stone

➤

DAMASCUS GATE

BEAR AND HIS DAUGHTER:
STORIES

OUTERBRIDGE REACH

CHILDREN OF LIGHT

A FLAG FOR SUNRISE

DOG SOLDIERS

A HALL OF MIRRORS

BEAR AND HIS DAUGHTER

➤

STORIES

➤

Robert Stone

A MARINER BOOK
HOUGHTON MIFFLIN COMPANY
BOSTON • NEW YORK

First Mariner Books edition 1998

Copyright © 1997 by Robert Stone
ALL RIGHTS RESERVED

For information about permission to reproduce selections
from this book, write to Permissions, Houghton Mifflin Company,
215 Park Avenue South, New York, New York 10003.

Library of Congress Cataloging-in-Publication Data
Stone, Robert.
Bear and his daughter : stories / Robert Stone.
p.   cm.
Contents: Miserere — Absence of mercy — Porque no tiene,
porque le falta — Helping — Under the pitons — Aquarius
obscured — Bear and his daughter.
ISBN 0-395-63652-3
ISBN 0-395-90134-0 (pbk.)
I. Title.
PS3569.T6418B43 1997
813'.54 — dc20   96-36737 CIP

Printed in the United States of America

Book design by Robert Overholtzer

EB 10 9 8 7 6 5 4 3

The following stories in this collection originally appeared
elsewhere: "Miserere," *The New Yorker;* "Absence of Mercy,"
Harper's Magazine; "Porque No Tiene, Porque Le Falta,"
New American Review; "Helping," *The New Yorker;* "Under
the Pitons," *Esquire;* "Aquarius Obscured,"
American Review.

for JANICE

Contents

MISERERE

MARY URQUHART had just finished story hour at the library when the muted phone rang at the circulation desk. She had been reading the children *Prince Caspian*.

Camille Innaurato was on the line and as usual she was beside herself.

"Mary, Mary, so listen . . ." Camille began. It sounded almost prayerful. Then Camille began to hyperventilate.

"Oh, Camille," Mrs. Urquhart said. "Try to be calm. Are you all right, dear? Do you have your inhaler?"

"I have more!" Camille croaked fiercely at last. The force of the words in her constricted throat made her sound, Mary Urquhart thought, like her counterpart in *Traviata*.

"More?" Although Mary knew at once what Camille meant, she needed the extra moment of freedom.

"More babies!" Camille shouted. She spoke so loudly that even with the receiver as close to her ear as she could bear, Mary Urquhart thought that everyone around the circulation desk must be able to hear her voice on the phone, its unsound passion.

"My brother, he found them!" cried Camille. "And he took them here. So I got them now."

"I see," said Mary Urquhart.

Outside, Mrs. Carter, the African-American head librarian, was supervising the reuniting of the story-hour children with their mothers. The children were, without exception, black and Hispanic. The mothers of the black children were mostly West Indian domestics; they were the most scrupulous of the story-hour mothers and they loved their children to have English stories, British stories.

"Mary . . ." Camille gasped over the phone. "Mary?"

Outside the library windows, in the darkening winter afternoon, the children looked lively and happy and well behaved and Mary was proud of them. The mothers were smiling, and Mrs. Carter too.

"Easy does it," said Mary Urquhart to her friend Camille. For years after Mary had stopped drinking, she had driven around with a bumper sticker to that effect. Embarrassing to consider now.

"You'll come, Mary? You could come today? Soon? And we could do it?"

The previous year Mrs. Urquhart had bought little books of C. S. Lewis tales with her own money for the children to take home. That way at least some might learn to read them. She liked to meet the mothers herself and talk with them. Looking on wistfully, she wished herself out on the sidewalk too, if only to say hello and remind herself of everyone's name. But Mrs. Carter was the chief librarian and preempted the privilege of overseeing the dismissal of story hour.

"Yes, dear," Mary said to Camille. "I'll come as soon as we close."

They closed within the hour because the New Jersey city in which Mary worked had scant funds to spare for libraries. It was largely a city of racial minorities, in the late stages of passing from the control of a corrupt white political machine to that of a corrupt black one. Its schools were warrens of pathology and patronage. Its police, still mainly white, were frequently criminals.

Mary Urquhart looked carefully about her as she went out the door into the library parking lot for the walk to her old station wagon. It was nearly night, though a faint stain of the day persisted. At the western horizon, across the river and over the stacks and gables of the former mills, hung a brilliant patch of clear night sky where Venus blazed. Some of the newer street lights around the library's block were broken, their fixtures torn away by junkies for sale to scrap dealers. There were patchy reefs and banks of soiled frozen snow on the ground. Not much had fallen for a week, but the weather was bitter and the north-facing curbs and margins were still partly covered.

"Thou fair-haired angel of the evening," Mary recited silently to the first star. She could not keep the line from her mind.

Temple Street, the road Mary drove toward the strip that led her home, was one of crumbling wooden houses. In some of them, bare lights glowed behind gypsy-colored bedspreads tacked over the taped windows. About every fifth house was derelict and inside some of these candlelight was already flickering. They were crack houses. Mary had worked as an enumerator in the neighborhood during the last census and, for all its transience, she knew it fairly well. Many of the houses were in worse condition inside than out. The official census description for all of them was "Dilapidated." A few of her story children lived on the street.

The odd corner had a bodega in a cinderblock building with a faint neon beer sign in its window. The cold had driven the brown-bagging drinkers away from the little strip mall that housed Mashona's Beauty Shoppe, a cheap lamp store and a takeout ribs joint called Floyd's, which kept erratic hours. All the shops closed at dusk and God knew, she thought, where the alcoholics had gone. Maybe out of the bitter wind into the crack houses. Mary knew a lot of the older alcoholics who hung out there by sight and sometimes, in daytime, she stopped for Floyd's ribs, which were not at all bad. Floyd, who always had a smile for her, kept a sign over his register that read CHRIST IS THE ANSWER.

She had an ongoing dialogue with a few of the men. Those who would speak to a middle-aged white woman like herself called her "Mary" and sometimes, in the case of the beat old-timers from down home, "Miss Mary." She had begun by addressing them all as "sir," but she had soon perceived that this offended them as patronizing and was not appropriate to street banter. So, if she did not know them by name, she addressed them as "guy," which amused them. It was how her upper-class Southern husband had addressed his social equals. He had used it long before one heard it commonly; he had been dead for thirteen years.

"I know your story, guy," she would say to a brown-bagging acquaintance as she carried her paper container of ribs to the car. "I'm a juicehead. I'm a boozer."

"But you gotta enjoy your life, Mary," an old man had said to her once. "You ain't got but one, chere?"

And that had stopped her cold.

"But that's it," she had told the man. "You're so right."

He had shaken his head, telling her really, well, she'd never understand. Her life and his? But she'd persisted.

"That's why I don't have my bottle today as you do. Because there was a time, guy. Yes, you best believe it."

Then he'd heard her vestigial Southernness and cocked his head and said, in a distinctly sarcastic but not altogether un-friendly way, "Do it right, Mary. You say so."

"God bless, guy."

"Be right, Mary."

Poor fellow, she'd thought. Who was he? Who might he have become? She wished him grace.

A short distance before Temple Street doglegged into the strip of Route 4, it passed the dangerous side of a city park in which there was a large lake. The cold weather had frozen the lake to a depth that Mary knew must be many feet. After the cold weeks they'd had, it must be safe for skating. In some towns there would be lights by the lakeside and skating children; not in this one. And for that she could only be grateful, because she did not think she could bear the sight of children skating or lights on the icy surface of a frozen lake. Even after the thirteen years.

Along its last quarter mile, Temple Street acquired an aluminum guardrail and some halogen overhead lights, though on these, too, the metal was torn up, unscrewed, pried loose by the locust-junkies.

At the light that marked the intersection with Route 4 stood a large gas station. It was one of a number owned by an immigrant from India. Once the immigrant himself had worked in it, then he'd bought it, then bought others and real estate to go with them. Now he employed other Indian immigrants who worked long shifts, day and night. In the previous twelve months, according to the county newspaper, no fewer than four of the immigrants had been shot dead in holdups and another four wounded.

Mary waited at the light, and it was really easier to think about the poor slaughtered Gujaratis than about the frozen lake. She prayed for them, in her way, eyes focused on the turn signal. It did not suit her to utter repetitions. Rather the words came to her on all the music she had heard, so many settings, that prayer sung over and over since the beginning of music itself.

> Agnus Dei, qui tollis peccata mundi,
> Miserere nobis.

Then there was Route 4, the American Strip. And this was New Jersey, where she had ended up, its original home and place of incubation, whence it had been nourished to creep out and girdle the world. It had come in time to her own stately corner of North Carolina, looking absolutely the same.

Since her widowhood and recovery, Mary Urquhart had lived in a modest house in what had once been a suburb of this New Jersey city, only a few blocks beyond its formal border. At the suburban end of her street was a hill from which the towers of Manhattan were visible on the clearer mornings. All day and most of the night, planes on a southward descent for Newark passed overhead and, even after so many years, often woke her.

But Mary was not, that afternoon, on her way home. A mile short of the city line, she pulled off Route 4 onto Imperial Avenue. The avenue led to a neighborhood called Auburn Hill, which had become an Italian enclave in the Spanish-speaking section of the ghetto. Auburn Hill could be relied upon for neat lawns and safe streets, their security reinforced by grim anecdotes of muggers' and housebreakers' summary punishments. Young outlaws nailed to tar rooftops with screwdrivers. Or thrown from an overpass onto the Jersey Central tracks fifty feet below. At Christmastime, the neighborhood sparkled with cheery lights. Mary had come to know it well and, comprehending both the bitter and the sweet of Auburn Hill, was fond of it.

Camille Innaurato's was like the other houses in that end of town. It was a brick, three-bedroom single-story with aluminum siding and a narrow awning of the same. It had a small lawn in front, surrounded by a metal fence, and a garden in the back where Camille grew tomatoes and peppers in season.

When Mary pulled into the driveway, she saw Camille's pale, anxious face at the picture window. Camille was mouthing words, clasping her hands. In a moment she opened the door to the winter wind, as Mary emerged from her car and locked it.

"Oh, Mary. I'm thanking God Almighty you could come. Yeah, I'm thanking him."

Camille was one of those women who had grown older in unquestioning service to her aged parents. She had helped raise her younger brother. Later she had shared with her father the care of her sick mother. Then, when he died, she had assumed it all — her mother, the house, everything. Camille worked in a garment-sewing shop that had set itself up on two floors of a former silk mill; she oversaw the Chinese and Salvadoran women employed there.

Her younger brother, August, was technically a policeman, though not an actively corrupt one. In fact, he had no particular constabulary duties. The family had had enough political connections to secure him a clerical job with the department. He was a timid, excitable man, married, with grown children, who lived with his domineering wife in an outer suburb. But as a police insider he knew the secrets of the city.

The Innauratos, brother and sister, had inherited nothing from their parents except the house Camille occupied and their sick mother's tireless piety.

Mary Urquhart stepped inside and took Camille by the shoulders and looked at her.

"Now, Camille, dear, are you all right? Can you breathe?"

She inspected Camille and, satisfied with her friend's condition, checked out the house. The living room was neat enough, although the television set was off, a sure sign of Camille's preoccupation.

"I gotta show you, Mary. Oh I gotta show you. Yeah I gotta." She sounded as though she were weeping, but the beautiful dark eyes she fixed on Mary were dry. Eyes out of Alexandrian portraiture, Mary thought, sparkling and shimmering with their infernal vision. For a moment it seemed she had returned from some transport. She gathered Mary to her large, soft, barren breast. "You wanna coffee, Mary honey? You wanna *biscote?* A little of wine?"

In her excitement, Camille always offered the wine when there were babies, forgetting Mary could not drink it.

"I'll get you a glass of wine," Mary suggested. "And I'll get myself coffee."

Camille looked after Mary anxiously as she swept past her toward the kitchen.

"Sit down, dear," Mary called to her. "Sit down and I'll bring it out."

Slowly, Camille seated herself on the edge of the sofa and stared at the blank television screen.

In the immaculate kitchen, Mary found an open bottle of sangiovese, unsoured, drinkable. She poured out a glass, then served herself a demitasse of fresh-made espresso from Camille's machine. In the cheerless, spotless living room, they drank side by side on the faded floral sofa, among the lace and the pictures of Camille's family and the portrait photograph of the Pope.

"I used to love sangiovese," Mary said, watching her friend sip. "The wine of the Romagna. Bologna. Urbino."

"It's good," Camille said.

"My husband and I and the children once stayed in a villa outside Urbino. It rained. Yes, every day, but the mountains were grand. And the hill towns down in Umbria. We had great fun."

"You saw the Holy Father?"

Mary laughed. "We were all good Protestants then."

Camille looked at her in wonder, though she had heard the story of Mary's upbringing many times. Then her face clouded.

"You gotta see the babies, Mary."

"Yes," Mary sighed. "But do finish your wine."

When the wine was done they both went back to look at the

fetuses. There were four. Camille had laid them on a tarpaulin, under a churchy purple curtain on the floor of an enclosed, unheated back porch, where it was nearly as cold as the night outside. On top of the curtain she had rested one of her wall crucifixes.

Mary lifted the curtain and looked at the little dead things on the floor. They had lobster-claw, unseparated fingers, and one had a face. Its face looked like a Florida manatee's, Mary thought. It was the only living resemblance she could bring to bear — a manatee, bovine, slope-browed. One was still enveloped in some kind of fibrous membrane that suggested bat wings.

"So sweet," Camille sobbed. "So sad. Who could do such a thing? A murderer!" She bit her thumb. "A murderer, the degenerate fuck, his eyes should be plucked out!" She made the sign of the cross, to ask forgiveness for her outburst.

"Little lamb, who made thee?" Mary Urquhart asked wearily. The things were so disgusting. "Well, to work then."

Camille's brother August had discovered that the scavenger company that handled the county's medical waste also serviced its abortion clinics, which had no incinerators of their own. The fetuses were stored for disposal along with everything else. August had fixed it with the scavengers to report specimens and set them aside. He would pass on the discovery to Camille. Then Camille and a friend — most often Mary — would get to work.

Mary knew a priest named Father Hooke, the pastor of a parish in a wealthy community in the Ramapos. They had known each other for years. Hooke had been, in a somewhat superficial way, Mary's spiritual counselor. He was much more cultivated than most priests and could be wickedly witty, too. Their conversations about contemporary absurdities, Scripture and the vagaries of the Canon, history and literature had helped her through the last stage of her regained abstinence. She knew of Julian of Norwich through his instruction. He had received her into the Catholic Church and she had been a friend to him. Lately, though, there had been tension between them. She used Camille's telephone to alert him.

"Frank," she said to the priest, "we have some children."

He gave her silence in return.

"Hello, Frank," she said again. "Did you hear me, Father? I said we have some children."

"Yes," said Hooke, in what Mary was coming to think of as his affected tone, "I certainly heard you the first time. Tonight is . . . difficult."

"Yes, it surely is," Mary said. "Difficult and then some. When will you expect us?"

"I've been meaning," Hooke said, "to talk about this before now."

He had quoted Dame Julian to her. "All shall be well, and all shall be well, and all manner of thing shall be well." Those were lines he liked.

"Have you?" she inquired politely. "I see. We can talk after the interment."

"You know, Mary," Father Hooke said with a nervous laugh, "the bishop, that pillar of intellect, our spiritual prince, has been hearing things that trouble him."

Mary Urquhart blushed to hear the priest's lie.

"The bishop," she told him, "is not a problem in any way. You are."

"Me?" He laughed then, genuinely and bitterly. "I'm a problem? Oh, sorry. There are also a few laws . . ."

"What time, Father? Camille works for a living. So do I."

"The thing is," Father Hooke said, "you ought not to come tonight."

"Oh, Frank," Mary said. "Really, really. Don't be a little boy on me. Take up your cross, guy."

"I suppose," Hooke said, "I can't persuade you to pass on this one?"

"Shame on you, Frank Hooke," she said.

The drive to the clean outer suburbs led through subdivisions and parklands, then to thick woods among which colonial houses stood, comfortably lighted against the winter night. Finally there were a few farms, or estates laid out to resemble working farms. The woods were full of frozen lakes and ponds.

The Buick wagon Mary drove was almost fifteen years old, the same one she had owned in the suburbs of Boston as a youngish mother, driving all the motherly routes, taking Charles Junior to soccer practice and Payton to girls' softball and little Emily to play school.

The fetuses were secured with blind cord in the back of the station wagon, between the tarp and the curtain in which Camille had wrapped them. It was a cargo that did not shift or rattle and they had not tried to put a crucifix on top. More and more, the dark countryside they rode through resembled the town where she had lived with Charles and her children.

"Could you say the poem?" Camille asked. When they went on an interment Camille liked to hear Mary recite poetry for her as they drove. Mary preferred poetry to memorized prayer, and the verse was always new to Camille. It made her cry, and crying herself out on the way to an interment, Mary had observed, best prepared Camille for the work at hand.

"But which poem, Camille?"

Sometimes Mary recited Crashaw's "To the Infant Martyrs," or from his hymn to Saint Teresa. Sometimes she recited Vaughan or Blake.

"The one with the star," Camille said. "The one with the lake."

"Oh," Mary said cheerfully. "Funny, I was thinking about it earlier."

Once, she could not imagine how, Mary had recited Blake's "To the Evening Star" for Camille. It carried such a weight of pain for her that she dreaded its every line and trembled when it came to her unsummoned:

> Thou fair-hair'd angel of the evening,
> Now, whilst the sun rests on the mountains, light
> Thy bright torch of love; thy radiant crown
> Put on, and smile upon our evening bed!

It had almost killed her to recite it the first time, because that had been her and Charles's secret poem, their prayer for the protection that was not forthcoming. The taste of it in her mouth was of rage unto madness and the lash of grief and above all of whiskey to drown it all, whiskey to die in and be with them. That night, driving, with the dark dead creatures at their back, she offered up the suffering in it.

Camille wept at the sound of the words. Mary found herself unable to go on for a moment.

"There's more," Camille said.

"Yes," said Mary. She drew upon her role as story lady.

> Let thy west wind sleep on
> The lake; speak silence with thy glimmering eyes,
> And wash the dusk with silver. Soon, full soon,
> Dost thou withdraw; then the wolf rages wide,
> And the lion glares thro' the dun forest:
> The fleeces of our flocks are cover'd with
> Thy sacred dew: protect them with thine influence.

Camille sobbed. "Oh Mary," she said. "Yours weren't protected."

"Well, stars . . ." Mary Urquhart said, still cheerfully. "Thin influence. Thin ice."

The parlor lights were lighted in the rectory of Our Lady of

Fatima when they pulled off the genteel main street of the foot-hill town and into the church parking lot. Mary parked the station wagon close to the rectory door, and the two women got out and rang Father Hooke's bell.

Hooke came to the door in a navy cardigan, navy-blue shirt and chinos. Camille murmured and fairly curtsied in deference. Mary looked the priest up and down. His casual getup seemed like recalcitrance, an unreadiness to officiate. Had he been working himself up to deny them?

"Hello, Frank," said Mary. "Sorry to come so late."

Hooke was alone in the rectory. There was no assistant and he did his own housekeeping, resident rectory biddies being a thing of the past.

"Can I give you coffee?" Father Hooke asked.

"I've had mine," Mary said.

He had a slack, uneasy smile. "Mary," the priest said. "And Miss . . . won't you sit down?"

He had forgotten Camille's name. He was a snob, she thought, a suburban snob. The ethnic, Mariolatrous name of his parish, Our Lady of Fatima, embarrassed him.

"Father," she said, "why don't we just do it?"

He stared at her helplessly. Ashamed for him, she avoided his eye.

"I think," he said, dry-throated, "we should consider from now on."

"Isn't it strange?" she asked Camille. "I had an odd feeling we might have a problem here tonight." She turned on Hooke. "What do you mean? Consider what?"

"All right, all right," he said. A surrender in the pursuit of least resistance. "Where is it?"

"They," Mary said.

"The babies," said Camille. "The poor babies are in Mary's car outside."

But he hung back. "Oh, Mary," said Father Hooke. He seemed childishly afraid.

She burned with rage. Was there such a thing as an adult Catholic? And the race of priests, she thought, these self-indulgent, boneless men.

"Oh, dear," she said. "What can be the matter now? Afraid of how they're going to look?"

"Increasingly . . ." Father Hooke said, "I feel we're doing something wrong."

"Really?" Mary asked. "Is that a fact?" They stood on the edge of the nice red Bolivian rectory carpet, in the posture of setting out for the station wagon. Yet not setting out. There was Haitian art on the wall. No lace curtains here. "What a shame," she said, "we haven't time for an evening of theological discourse."

"We may have to make time," Father Hooke said. "Sit down, girls."

Camille looked to Mary for reassurance and sat with absurd decorousness on the edge of a bare-boned Spanish chair. Mary stood where she was. The priest glanced at her in dread. Having giving them an order, he seemed afraid to take a seat himself.

"It isn't just the interments," he told Mary. He ignored Camille. "It's the whole thing. Our whole position." He shuddered and began to pace up and down on the rug, his hands working nervously.

"Our position," Mary repeated tonelessly. "Do you mean your position? Are you referring to the Church's teaching?"

"Yes," he said. He looked around as though for help, but as was the case so often with such things, it was not available. "I mean I think we may be wrong."

She let the words reverberate in the rectory's quiet. Then she asked, "Prodded by conscience, are you, Father?"

"I think we're wrong on this," he said with sudden force. "I think women have a right. I do. Sometimes I'm ashamed to wear my collar."

She laughed her pleasant, cultivated laughter. "Ashamed to wear your collar? Poor Frank. Afraid people will think badly of you?"

He summoned anger. "Kindly spare me the ad hominem," he said.

"But Frank," she said, it seemed lightly, "there is only ad hominem."

"I'm afraid I'm not theologian enough," he said, "to follow you there."

"Oh," said Mary, "I'm sorry, Father. What I mean in my crude way is that what is expected of you is expected personally. Expected directly. Of *you*, Frank."

He sulked. A childish resentful silence. Then he said, "I can't believe God wants us to persecute these young women the way you people do. I mean you particularly, Mary, with your so-called counseling."

He meant the lectures she gave the unwed mothers who were referred to her by pamphlet. Mary had attended anti-war and anti-apartheid demonstrations with pride. The abortion clinic demonstrations she undertook as an offered humiliation, standing among the transparent cranks and crazies as a penance and a curb to pride. But surprisingly, when she was done with them in private, over coffee and cake, many pregnant women brought their pregnancies to term.

She watched Father Hooke. He was without gravitas, she thought. The hands, the ineffectual sputter.

"For God's sake," he went on, "look at the neighborhood where you work! Do you really think the world requires a few million more black, alienated, unwanted children?"

She leaned against one of his antique chests and folded her

arms. She was tall and elegant, as much an athlete and a beauty at fifty as she had ever been. Camille sat open-mouthed.

"How contemptible and dishonest of you to pretend an attack of conscience," she told Hooke quietly. "It's respectability you're after. And to talk about what God wants?" She seemed to be politely repressing a fit of genuine mirth. "When you're afraid to go out and look at his living image? Those things in the car, Frank, that poor little you are afraid to see. That's man, guy, those little forked purple beauties. That's God's image, don't you know that? That's what you're scared of."

He took his glasses off and blinked helplessly.

"Your grief . . ." he began. A weakling, she thought, trying for the upper hand. Trying to appear concerned. In a moment he had lost his nerve. "It's made you cruel . . . Maybe not *cruel,* but . . ."

Mary Urquhart pushed herself upright. "Ah," she said with a flutter of gracious laughter, "the well-worn subject of my grief. Maybe I'm drunk again tonight, eh Father? Who knows?"

Thirteen years before on the lake outside Boston, on the second evening before Christmas, her husband had taken the children skating. First young Charley had wanted to go and Charles had demurred; he'd had a few drinks. Then he had agreed in his shaggy, teasing, slow-spoken way — he was rangy, wry, a Carolina Scot like Mary. It was almost Christmas and the kids were excited and how long would it stay cold enough to skate? Then Payton had demanded to go, and then finally little Emily, because Charles had taught them to snap the whip on ice the day before. And the lake, surrounded by woods, was well lighted and children always skated into the night although there was one end, as it turned out, where the light failed, a lonely bay bordered with dark blue German pine where even then maybe some junkie had come out from Roxbury or Southie or Lowell or God knew where and destroyed the light for the metal around it. And Emily still had her cold and should not have gone.

But they went and Mary waited late, and sometimes, listening to music, having a Wild Turkey, she thought she heard voices sounding strange. She could remember them perfectly now, and the point where she began to doubt, so faintly, that the cries were in fun.

The police said he had clung to the ice for hours, keeping himself alive and the children clinging to him, and many people had heard the calling out but taken it lightly.

She was there when the thing they had been was raised, a blue cluster wrapped in happy seasonal colors, woolly reindeer hats and scarves and mittens, all grasping and limbs intertwined, and it looked, she thought, like a rat king, the tangle of rats trapped together in their own naked tails and flushed from an abandoned hull to float drowned, a raft of solid rat on the swells of the lower Cape Fear River. The dead snarls on their faces, the wild eyes, a paradigm she had seen once as a child she saw again in the model of her family. And near Walden Pond, no less, the west wind slept on the lake, eyes glimmered in the silver dusk, a dusk at morning. She had lost all her pretty ones.

"Because," she said to Father Hooke, "it would appear to me that you are a man — and I know men, I was married to a man — who is a little boy, a little boy-man. A tiny boy-man, afraid to touch the cross or look in God's direction."

He stared at her and swallowed. She smiled as though to reassure him.

"What you should do, Father, is this. Take off the vestments you're afraid to wear. Your mama's dead for whom you became a priest. Become the nice little happy homosexual nonentity you are."

"You are a cruel bitch," Hooke said, pale-faced. "You're a sick and crazy woman."

Camille in her chair began to gasp. Mary bent to attend her.
"Camille? Do you have your inhaler?"

Camille had it. Mary helped her adjust it and waited until her friend's breathing was under control. When she stood up, she saw that Father Hooke was in a bad way.

"You dare," Mary said to him, "you wretched tiny man, to speak of black unwanted children? Why, there is not a suffering black child — God bless them all — not a black child in this unhappy foolish country that I would not exalt and nourish on your goddamn watery blood. I would not risk the security of the most doomed, lost, deformed black child for your very life, you worthless pussy!"

Father Hooke had become truly upset. My Lord, she thought, now I've done it. Now I'll see the creature cry. She looked away.

"You were my only friend," Father Hooke told her when he managed to speak again. "Did you know that?"

She sighed. "I'm sorry, Father. I suppose I have my ignorant cracker side and God help me I am sick and I am crazy and cruel. Please accept my sincerest apologies. Pray for me."

Hooke would not be consoled. Kind-hearted Camille, holding her inhaler, took a step toward him as though she might help him somehow go on breathing.

"Get out," he said to them. "Get out before I call the police."

"You have to try to forgive me, Charles." Had she called him Charles? How very strange. Poor old Charles would turn in his grave. "Frank, I mean. You have to try and forgive me, Frank. Ask God to forgive me. I'll ask God to forgive you. We all need it, don't we, Father."

"The police!" he cried, his voice rising. "Because those things, those goddamn things in your car! Don't you understand? People accuse us of violence!" he shouted. "And you are violence!" Then he more or less dissolved.

She went and put a hand on his shoulder as Camille watched in amazement.

"God forgive us, Frank." But he leaned on the back of his leather easy chair and turned from her, weeping. "Oh Frank, you lamb," she said, "what did your poor mama tell you? Did she say that a world with God was easier than one without him?"

She gave Father Hooke a last friendly pat and turned to Camille. "Because that would be mistaken, wouldn't it, Camille?"

"Oh, you're right," Camille hastened to say. The tearful priest had moved her too. But still she was dry-eyed, staring, Alexandrian. "You're so right, Mary."

When they were on the road again it was plain Camille Innaurato was exhausted.

"So, Mary," she asked. "So where're we going now, honey?"

"Well," Mary said, "as it happens, I have another fella up my sleeve." She laughed. "Yes, another of these worthies Holy Mother Church provides for our direction. Another selfless man of the cloth."

"I'll miss Mass tomorrow."

"This is Mass," Mary said.

"Right. OK."

This is Mass, she thought, this is the sacrifice nor are we out of it. She reached over and gave Camille a friendly touch.

"You don't work tomorrow, do you, love?"

"Naw, I don't," Camille said. "I don't, but . . ."

"I can take you home. I can get this done myself."

"No," said Camille, a little cranky with fatigue. "No way."

"Well, we'll get these children blessed, dear."

The man Mary had up her sleeve was a priest from Central Europe called Monsignor Danilo. It was after ten when Mary telephoned him from a service station, but he hurriedly agreed to do what she required. He was smooth and obsequious and seemed always ready to accommodate her.

His parish, St. Macarius, was in an old port town on Newark

Bay, and to get there they had to retrace their drive through the country and then travel south past several exits of the Garden State.

It took them nearly an hour, even with the sparse traffic. The church and its rectory were in a waterfront neighborhood of refineries and wooden tenements little better than the ones around Temple Street. The monsignor had arranged to meet them in the church.

The interior was an Irish-Jansenist nightmare of tarnished marble, white-steepled tabernacles and cream columns. Under a different patron, it had served the Irish dockers of a hundred years before. Its dimensions were too mean and narrow to support the mass of decoration, and Father Danilo's bunch had piled the space with their icons, vaguely Byzantine Slavic saints and Desert Fathers and celebrity saints in their Slavic aspect.

Candles were flickering as the two women entered. The place smelled of wax, stale wine and the incense of past ceremony. Mary carried the babies under their purple cloth.

Monsignor Danilo waited before the altar, at the end of the main aisle. He wore his empurpled cassock with surplice and a silk stole. His spectacles reflected the candlelight.

Beside him stood a tall, very thin, expressionless young man in cassock and surplice. The young man, in need of a shave, held a paten on which cruets of holy water and chrism and a slice of lemon had been set.

Monsignor Danilo smiled his lupine smile, and when Mary had set the babies down before the altar, he took her hand in his. In the past he had sometimes kissed it; tonight he pressed it to his breast. The intrusion of his flabby body on her senses filled Mary with loathing. He paid no attention to Camille Innaurato and he did not introduce the server.

"Ah," he said, bending to lift the curtain under which the creatures lay, "the little children, no?"

She watched him regard the things with cool compassion, as though he were moved by their beauty, their vestigial humanity, the likeness of their Creator. But perhaps, she thought, he had seen ghastly sights before and smiled on them. Innocent as he might be, she thought, he was the reeking model of every Jew-baiting, clerical fascist murderer who ever took orders east of the Danube. His merry countenance was crass hypocrisy. His hands were huge, thick-knuckled, the hands of a brute, as his face was the face of a smiling Cain.

"So beautiful," he said. Then he said something in his native language to the slovenly young man, who looked at Mary with a smirk and shrugged and smiled in a vulgar manner. She did not let her gaze linger.

Afterward, she would have to hear about Danilo's mother and her trip to behold the apparition of the Virgin in some Bessarabian or Balkan hamlet and the singular misfortunes, historically unique, of Danilo's native land. And she would have to give him at least seventy-five dollars or there would be squeals and a disappointed face. And now something extra for the young man, no doubt an illegal alien, jumped-ship and saving his pennies.

Camille Innaurato breathed through her inhaler. Father Danilo took a cruet from the paten and with his thick fingers sprinkled a blessing on the lifeless things. Then they all faced the altar and the Eastern crucifix that hung suspended there. They prayed together in the Latin each knew:

Agnus Dei, qui tollis peccata mundi,
Miserere nobis.

Finally, she was alone with the ancient Thing before whose will she still stood amazed, whose shadow and line and light they all were: the bad priest and the questionable young man and Camille Innaurato, she herself and the unleavened flesh fouling the floor. Adoring, defiant, in the crack-house flicker of that hideous, consecrated half-darkness, she offered It Its due, by old command.

Lamb of God, who takest away the sins of the world,
Have mercy on us.

ABSENCE OF MERCY

➤

MACKAY ONCE described himself as "the last orphan." He has a forlorn and humorous manner that makes his friends delight in the phrase. Some of them use it behind his back.

As a child of five, Mackay was sent to an institution operated by a Catholic order of teaching brothers. Though it was described as a boarding school, the male children who attended St. Michael's were all homeless to a greater or lesser degree, and many had lost, one way or another, both parents. About half had been enrolled by surviving relatives, who paid the Pauline Brothers a tuition that, in the mid-1940s, amounted to fifty dollars a year. Others had been placed there by the family-court system through the network of Catholic charities. The children were referred to, quaintly, as "scholars."

A significant minority of St. Michael's scholars were statutory delinquents. Many were suffering from emotional disturbances of varying severity. All were unhappy and unloved or unwisely loved or loved ineffectively. All were mildly malnourished; in later life, Mackay would find himself unable to remember the food at St. Michael's as food, only as the stuff of guilt or sickness. All were subject to unremitting petty violence.

To be a scholar at St. Michael's was to live on one's nerves. A good beating was forever at hand. Pale children were always whispering, their jaws rigid like ventriloquists', about surprise attacks, revenge and retribution. Sometimes it would seem to Mackay that his grade school years were a single continuous process of being found out in transgression and punished. At other times he would recall them as a physical and moral chaos of all against all.

Mackay had been placed in St. Michael's by reason of his mother's incapacity. His virgin aunt, a schoolteacher, paid the brothers. Mackay's mother was a single parent before her time and a paranoid schizophrenic. She was an educated, well-spoken woman, and Mackay could remember that in the years before their separate institutionalization she had often read to him. He could also remember lying with her in a dark room while music that was solemn and frightening played from an ornate wooden radio. Once in St. Michael's he forgot, for a while, his mother's face. He thought of her as a vague, troubled, tender presence. He was surprised, as an adult, to learn that she had been known to display a violent side.

Mackay's own experience of violence began at St. Michael's, where it appeared in three principal forms. The first was intramural, taking place among the scholars themselves and visited by the strong upon the weak. In obscure corners, in lavatories, showers and the swarming darkness after lights out, boys alone or in combinations fought out the laws of struggle and dominance. St. Michael was a warrior angel and St. Michael's Institute had the social dynamic of a coral reef.

In its second variation, violence was attendant upon the scholars' education and correction and was meted out from above by the brothers. Sometimes it was spontaneous and consisted of a clip, with or without a knuckle filling, to the head of a boy skylarking or talking in ranks. Idling in class, insufficiently complete answers to a teacher's question, or simply wrong ones, might also bring such an expression of displeasure. On one occasion, an unhappy arithmetic teacher lined up his entire third-grade class and slapped each scholar twice, hard across the face. Someone's slip of the tongue had provoked general unseemly laughter. The teacher, sardonically Mackay later believed, ordered his scholars to offer their humiliations to the Holy Ghost. The corporal punishment Mackay most dreaded was that administered formally, by the prefect of the primary school, with a worn razor strop. The smallest children and those in their first weeks at St. Michael's were not subject to such rigors, lax deportment in them being seen as the fruit of natural depravity. But for scholars aged six and over, the words "You will stand by my room . . . tonight!" uttered theatrically in the French-Canadian inflections of Brother Francis, prefect of the grammar school, were an occasion of stark, sick-making terror.

Finally, among the forms of violence, there were the weekly "smokers," in which a scholar found himself confronting both the authority of the institute and the mob spirit of his fellows. In the smokers, boys six and over were obliged to put on boxing gloves and flail away at each other for three two-minute rounds — time enough, Mackay discovered, to get beaten thoroughly. For years Mackay dreaded Thursday evenings and the smokers. In the middle of his second year, matched against a talented boy from West Virginia, he lost much of the hearing in one ear and years later discovered that his eardrum had been broken and his inner ear injured. Eventually he learned the requisite lessons. He learned to keep his head and to use his own anger. He learned to take blows, to take courage from someone else's show of pain and to use another's fear to his own advantage.

The necessity of accommodating the realities of conflict caused Mackay much inward confusion. He recalled and idealized his mother's gentleness like a lost kingdom, but pining about it would not do. Homesick brooding made him teary and vulnerable, which was a dangerous way to be. Struggle was the law. During his first years at St. Michael's, World War II was in progress. The war and the patriotic effort to fight it were presented at St. Michael's as having a sacred character. The war was an occasion of suffering and death, states that were well regarded there. Death was particularly sublime, the highest form of existence and a condition to be acquired as soon as responsibility permitted. The virtuous dead were the Church triumphant.

Mackay understood the weakness of his position. He felt that he required help from higher powers, but the higher powers seemed firmly on the side of Brother Francis, their earthly representative. Mackay's religious allegiances shifted with his daily fortunes. One day he would find himself in transports of love for his Father in Heaven, who was after all the only one he knew, and he would pray that God's will be done on earth. At other times he would desire nothing so much as the defeat and ruin of the United States, on the theory that even the conquering Japanese were bound to be an improvement on the Pauline Brothers. On such days he would address his prayers to Satan, Hitler and Stalin. It would seem at these times that the right side was not for him. Even today he seems to carry a strain of destructive skepticism in his nature, together with a strange credulity.

In the course of his time at St. Michael's, Mackay was able to laugh off much of the brothers' absent-minded battery. He joined a school gang, fought for and held a middling status in the primate democracy. He became a friend of one of the gang's principals, a red-headed boy named Christopher Kiernan, who excelled at the smokers. Mackay himself came to enjoy the smokers and even won a few. The statutory evening punishments he would never forgive or forget.

In the hours before lights out, there were always a few boys aged between six and nine standing in a line outside the cubicle in which the brother prefect slept. Besides serving as the House of Pain, the brother prefect's room was a place of great mystery, the only adult residence with which many of the scholars were familiar. Those who visited it most frequently would have been hard put to describe it, distracted as they were by their own fear and shame. Mackay remembers the white curtain, like a hospital screen, across the door and the smell of the brother prefect's pipe tobacco.

After the evening prayer and the bustle of innocent scholars retiring, the standers-by were left in semidarkness with the beating of their own hearts. Very occasionally, on the eve of holidays or simply at a whim, Brother Francis would commute the sentences of the condemned and send them scattering joyfully to bed. This remote possibility added a dimension of suspense to the nightly drama and enabled the children to experience the edifying sensation of vain hopes disappointed.

Ten minutes to a quarter of an hour after the lights had gone out, the prefect would emerge from behind his curtain and eye the quivering scholars like a high priest inspecting the offerings. He would then make a withering remark at their expense; one of his favorites was to address them as "mother's little darlings," a characterization hardly appropriate, since they were in fact orphans about to be beaten. Mackay always felt it directed at him in particular.

Then Brother Francis would return inside and consult his dreaded little black book and call the scholars in one by one. Punishment was administered in silence. It was expected to be endured with patience and to be, as the phrase went, "offered up." It was often pointed out at St. Michael's that Our Lord himself had cooperated with the authorities who put him to death, meekly obeying their commands in order that the sacrifice be accomplished. And the ceremonial nature of these punishments, the waiting in reverent silence and order, as though for a sacrament, the intensity of feeling undergone by the punished, all conspired to give an atmosphere of perverse religiosity to the business.

Pushing the curtain aside, a guilty scholar would enter the tiny room. Looming hugely overhead was the black-clad figure of Brother Francis. The razor strop was behind his back and he would hold it there until the victim extended a small left hand, palm upward. Three times the strop would descend, and after each blow the scholar, if he wanted to get it all over with, was required to offer his hand for the next. Mackay says he can remember the pain even today. After the left hand, it was time for three on the right.

The worst of it, Mackay says, was the absence of mercy. Once the punishment began, no amount of crying or pleading would stay the prefect's hand. Each blow followed upon the last, inexorably, like the will of God. It was the will of God. Brother Francis, implacable as a shark or a hurricane, carried out what was ordained on high. If a scholar withheld a trespassing hand, Brother Francis would wait until it was extended. He seemed to have nothing but time, like things themselves. Only in refusing to cry could a boy preserve a remnant of personal dignity. Mackay always tried to hold out. Once he made it through the second blow on the right hand before dissolving. It did not escape Mackay's notice that, in the end, everyone cried.

Duly punished, St. Michael's children would fly weeping toward their pillows, their burning hands tucked under their armpits, scuttling barefoot over the wooden floor like skinny little wingless birds. In bed, in the darkness, they would moan with pain and rage against the state of things, against Brother Francis and God's will, against their alcoholic fathers, feckless mothers or stepparents. Children can never imagine a suffering greater than their own.

Mackay was an intelligent child who liked books and so was able to mythologize his experience. One of the favorite myths informing his early childhood was the Dickensian one of the highborn orphan, fallen among brutish commoners. Sometimes he would try to identify and encourage in himself those traits of character that gave evidence of his lost eminence. The question of his own courage in the face of danger and enmity often occupied his thoughts. Years later, in navy boot camp, Mackay would discover that in the course of his years at St. Michael's he had acquired an instinctive cringe. This would be the first indication in adult life that he had not passed altogether unmarked through his early education.

When Mackay's mother was released from the hospital, Mackay left St. Michael's and went to live with her in a single bathless room at a welfare hotel on the West Side. He spent as much time as possible out of the room, on the street. In his second year of high school, he began to cut classes. He had become a "junior" of a West Side gang and spent much time drinking beer in Central Park at night and smoking, with a sense of abandon, the occasional reefer.

Once, in the dead hours of a summer night, he was drinking Scotch and Pepsi-Cola with four other youths around the Egyptian obelisk in Central Park called Cleopatra's Needle when a hostile band happened by. One of Mackay's friends had a knife, and in the fight that ensued a boy of the other party was stabbed. It was impossible to see everything in the darkness. The fight was almost silent. Mackay found that adrenaline worked against the sense of time; time advanced with his pulse beats, moment by moment. There was a cry of "Shank!" The stabbed boy cursed and groaned. At the height of the battle two mounted policemen from the Central Park precinct came galloping across the Great Lawn, bearing down on the combatants. Everyone scattered for cover.

Mackay and Chris Kiernan escaped over a wall and onto the

transverse road across the park at Seventy-ninth Street. There they found the teenager who had been stabbed, standing by the curb watching glassy-eyed as cars sped past him. He had been stabbed twice in the arm, warding off thrusts at his body. The wounds seemed deep and, Mackay thought, might well have killed had they been placed as intended.

The stabbed youth cursed them. Mackay and Kiernan felt compromised. Custom discouraged the promiscuous use of knives against white enemies. It seemed impossible to just leave him there, so they decided to help. Mackay and Kiernan made a tourniquet of his bloody white shirt. They walked him, talking encouragement, to the door of the nearest hospital, a luxurious private establishment off Madison Avenue. His shirt had become suffused with blood. Blood ran off his sneakers onto the pavement. As they approached the inner glass door of the hospital a man in white came forward from behind a reception desk and locked the door. When they protested, the man in white simply shook his head. Mackay and Kiernan somehow got the youth to Bellevue, left him outside Emergency and fled.

The following March, on St. Patrick's Day, Mackay was one of the drunken youths who, then as now, made the Upper East Side horrible with their carousing after the parade. His mother was back in the hospital and he was staying in an apartment in East Harlem with half a dozen other dropouts. Parents, not unwisely, cautioned their teenage children against association with him.

On the St. Patrick's Day in question, Mackay was drunk and unhappy. He picked a fight with his friend Kiernan in a poolroom on East Eighty-sixth Street. Kiernan, with what Mackay always felt was a lucky punch, stretched him out cold on the poolroom floor. He actually lay unconscious for a minute or two, whereupon the proprietors of the poolroom ejected him from the premises by throwing him down the many steps that led to the street. Mackay, tasting defeat, learned a certain embittered caution. Kiernan, on the other hand, came to regard his own belligerence too indulgently, as events years later would make clear.

In his last year of high school, Mackay joined the navy. He was fond of sea stories. He took the subway to South Ferry and signed the necessary papers in the offices at Whitehall Street, and by the end of the day he was on his way to the naval training center at Bainbridge, Maryland.

The navy Mackay joined in the mid-fifties was the navy of World War II, a tradition-minded, conservative service that prided itself on stiff discipline. It sought to produce individuals who could perform technical tasks under pressure, and its training procedures reflected this requirement. Every morning recruits turned out for inspection. It was summer and whites were the uniform of the day. The whites could not be machine washed or ironed. They were hand washed with a scrub brush and a bar of Ivory soap, then rolled in the regulation manner. If any part of a recruit's uniform was imperfectly washed or in some way out of order, the drill instructors would make him regret it.

In the second week of boot camp, during a performance of the manual of arms, a drill instructor named Igo discovered Mackay's cringe. Igo was a first-class boatswain's mate.

"My word!" Igo exclaimed. He enjoyed using this mild expletive because of the contrast it made with the rest of his vocabulary. "My word! This recruit has the attitude of a dog."

Mackay himself was surprised. He had never noticed himself cringing.

Igo took to addressing Mackay as "Pooch." He announced that he would drill the cringe out of him. He made things very unpleasant. Every morning after the training company was dismissed from inspection, Igo would drill him in the manual of arms.

"Here, Pooch," he would call amiably, to summon Mackay.

At one point Mackay told himself that if Igo called him Pooch once more, he would bash the boatswain's mate's brains out with his useless Springfield training rifle. He decided instead to interpret Igo's drilling as being in his own best interest. He had noticed that in the navy people were rarely actually struck; in that way the navy was unlike St. Michael's. He noticed also that the food was good, better than he had ever had anywhere.

Every morning he drilled with Igo. When they had gone through the manual of arms, Igo would menace him by waving a variety of objects over his head and try to catch him cringing. It was absurd and comical. Still, Mackay found it very hard to stare straight ahead and not to wince at the expected blows. Mackay thought of his cringe as a rat that lived near his heart, a rat with his own face. He hated it far worse than he hated Igo.

By the time he left boot camp for the fleet, he was able to stare the boatswain's mate down.

"Congratulations, sailor," Igo said to Mackay. "You're too scared to cringe."

Mastering the shameful reflex had been instructive, and Mackay never forgot it. He often wondered if everyone had a rat at his heart to kill.

Six years or so out of the navy, Mackay beheld himself a family man, married and the father of a baby boy. His mother was dead. Through good luck he was able to find a job as a photographer's assistant. Eventually the job would lead to his working as a news photographer and then to his becoming an artist, but it was a hard job with long hours and low pay. Mackay enjoyed it nonetheless and supplemented his income by working as a house painter. He lived with his family in a pleasant apartment on the West Side near Central Park. His wife was a graduate of the High School of Music and Art and of Reed College. Their friends were people of spirit and artistic interest. It was the early sixties and a good time to be young in New York. Mackay felt that the city in which he lived was a different city from the one in which he had grown up.

On a bright autumn Saturday Mackay walked over to Columbus Avenue for the morning paper and discovered that there was a picture of his old friend Chris Kiernan on the front page of the *Daily News*. The accompanying headline read: SAMARITAN KILLED IN SUBWAY SLAYING.

Kiernan had been riding the Seventh Avenue Express down from his in-laws' new apartment in the north Bronx. His Korean-American wife and their infant child were with him. At the 145th Street station a young man had boarded the train and begun harassing passengers. The young man was an unemployed immigrant from Ecuador and he had been drinking. He went through the cars from one end of the train to the other, making menacing gestures and cursing the subway riders in Spanish. Reaching the car in which Kiernan and his family were riding, he passed by them without comment. But in the same car he began to abuse a lone middle-aged woman. The woman looked at Kiernan, a big man with a practical face, plainly a husband and father, wearing a suit and tie. She called to him begging for help. As the train pulled into the 125th Street station, Kiernan went over to the young man and began to struggle with him. When the doors opened Kiernan wrestled him out onto the platform.

"You're getting off here," Kiernan was reported to have told the man. He gave the Ecuadorian a shove that sent him flying and returned to sit beside his wife. A ragged cheer went up.

The car doors should have closed then but they did not. Instead of continuing on to 116th Street, the train remained in the 125th Street station and the doors stayed open. Out on the platform the angry Ecuadorian struggled to his feet. According to witnesses, he went halfway up the stairs to the next level but then seemed to change his mind and came back down. Still the doors failed to close. The drunk young man got back on the express and stabbed Kiernan through the heart. Kiernan stood up and tried to chase him. The man fled up the stairs. Kiernan fell dead on the station platform in what the *Daily News* described as "a pool of blood."

Mackay stood transfixed on the corner of Columbus Avenue in the rare autumn sunshine reading about Kiernan's murder. He and Chris Kiernan had known each other since they were both six years old. The *Daily News* story mentioned the fact that Kiernan had once been a scholar at St. Michael's. He had gone on to attend St. Peter's College in New Jersey and later became an army officer. At the time of his death he was an account executive at Batten, Barton, Durstine and Osborn. His friends were quoted regarding his excellence of character.

Mackay was shaken. A thrill of fear went through him as he picked up the *Times* and paid for both papers and started home. Although they had not seen each other for ten years they had once been very close. They had suffered shame and pain together that could never be explained to anyone. They were of the same stuff. Mackay felt his existence threatened by Kiernan's death. He felt diminished.

In Albany, a legislator introduced a bill to benefit the survivors of people who incurred injury or death assisting their fellow citizens in an emergency. It was referred to as the "Christopher Kiernan Bill." Reading about it all, Mackay smiled uncomfortably and shook his head. Kiernan had always had naive notions of high life. He was terribly ashamed of his origins and even ashamed of his Irish name. He had dressed in a collegiate manner and attempted to eliminate his New York accent. Mackay believed that Kiernan would have changed his face if he could. Like Mackay, he had wanted to leave a great deal behind. How he would have hated the Tammany politician's "Christopher Kiernan Bill," Mackay thought. How he must have hated to die in the subway.

It occurred to Mackay over the weekend that he ought somehow to honor Kiernan's memory. He thought about going to the funeral, about writing to Kiernan's wife or stopping by the wake to sign the book. In the end he did nothing. He did not want the world of his childhood to touch him. He wanted it gone, buried with Kiernan. It seemed to him that Kiernan would have been the first to understand.

Afterward Mackay would wonder if the bits and pieces of violence he and Kiernan had lived out together had not conditioned the future and led Kiernan to his death. He suspected that past successes had encouraged Kiernan to action. Of course, it had been the right thing, the brave thing. But in spite of his horror, Mackay felt himself considering Kiernan's undoing with a fascination that might be mistaken for guilty satisfaction.

One thing he knew for certain was that he wanted no part of violence anymore, on any scale. He swore that he would never strike his children or allow them to be hit by anyone. He adopted a mode of politics he believed would place him in opposition to war. He felt a deep commitment to the good causes of the sixties. He felt as though he had earned the right to work for peace and human brotherhood. He embraced those things with joy.

Mackay could not know then that he would one day take a coarse satisfaction in the middle-class elegance of his grown children, whom he would raise in an atmosphere of progressive right-mindedness that would present them with problems of their own. Or that he would brag to them of the rigors of his own upbringing. His life was not to be the irresistible moral progress for which he might have hoped.

The year after Kiernan's death, Mackay was painting and papering an apartment on Jane Street. About four in the afternoon on a Thursday in March, the first warm spring day of the year, he walked to the Fourteenth Street station and boarded the IRT uptown express for home. A few minutes later he got out at Seventy-second Street to change for the local train.

Standing near him on the platform was an elderly woman in a black cloth coat. She appeared very frail and a little confused. Mackay, perhaps thinking of his mother, felt well disposed toward her.

A tall, fair-skinned man in a light-colored plaid suit came walking down the platform. For some reason, Mackay noticed him at once. The man was whistling between his teeth as he went. He seemed to be looking for someone. His manner was ebullient. Every once in a while he would stop and appear to chat with someone waiting for the local. The people addressed would either look away or simply stare at him expressionless. He had gray hair, a lean foxy face and lively blue eyes.

As Mackay watched, the man approached the elderly woman nearby. Mackay saw him speak to her and saw her look away. The man appeared to be delivering himself of some casual pleasantry, but the woman ignored him and moved down the platform. The tall man followed her, smiling, and spoke to her again. At first Mackay thought that the two must know each other. Then he saw that the woman was frightened. She tried to step around the man and move toward Mackay. The man blocked her way and laughed. Mackay could not hear the words the tall man spoke but he heard the laugh. It was loud and witless. The elderly woman turned her back on her tormentor, hugging her pocketbook close. The laughing man stepped around to face her. Mackay drew nearer and quietly moved where he could see the old woman's face. He saw it convulsed with fear, sheeplike, vacant and repellent. The man reached out and touched an ornament on the woman's coat collar.

The Seventy-second Street IRT station was the one from which Mackay, not yet dispossessed of his cringe, had set out to enlist in the navy. Its platforms were narrow. Its stairways ascended from the middle of the platform to form a central pyramid, so that there was really only one way out. Fifteen feet from where he stood, Mackay saw the old woman begin to cry. She was trying to pull away. The man held her by the coat ornament. Her loose aged lips were trembling. The platform was crowded with people but, looking about him again, Mackay realized that no one else was watching.

Mackay stepped forward. He still hoped that somehow the situation would unmake itself, that some word or action would occur to show its normalcy and innocence. Just before intervening, Mackay took a last decisive look at the man on the platform. What he saw gave him pause. Although he was a day or two unshaven, there was something rather distinguished about the man's appearance. His bearing was firm and confident. His features were delicate and more pleasant than otherwise. He was neatly and tastefully dressed in a jacket and tie. His hair was wavy and slightly long in the back like an old-fashioned Middle European musician's. His eyes were happy, although wide and staring.

"Anything wrong?" Mackay asked the elderly woman. She looked at him in desperation.

When the tall man turned to him, Mackay saw that the man was sturdier and younger than he had appeared at a distance. He was looking at Mackay in blue-eyed amazement.

"You!" he said. As though he knew Mackay and recognized him. "You!" the man half screamed. His cry of recognition seemed to transcend the merely personal. He seemed indeed to be recognizing in the person of Mackay everything that had ever been wrong with his life, which Mackay suspected had been quite a lot.

Out of the corner of his eye, Mackay saw the woman who had been menaced edging away.

"Take a walk," Mackay told the man sternly. Immediately

he regretted the pathetic suburban bravado of his words. In his own ears his voice had the quality of a dream. It was as though, upon addressing the man, he had entered something like a dream state. Events thereafter seemed lit in an unnatural light.

"You are from Doc," the man said. He spoke with a Germanic accent. At first it sounded as though he had said, "You are from God." When the man repeated it, Mackay got it straight. "You are from Doc."

Mackay saw the unnatural brightness of his eyes and the starvation gauntness of his bony face. It was frightening to imagine what kind of life had to be endured behind such eyes. They were without order or justice or reason. For a moment, the two men stood motionless on the platform, facing each other. Mackay listened to the older man's shrill dreamlike laughter.

"You are an English queer," the man said to Mackay and attacked him.

When Mackay raised his fists the man slipped easily around his guard. Like an inexperienced fighter, Mackay had raised his chin contentiously. The man punched him in the throat and for a moment he could not draw breath. He stepped back in confusion, then quickly decided he was unhurt. The man came at him again.

Grappling hand to hand, Mackay realized with horror his opponent's strength. His first impression of the older man's age and fragility had been mistaken altogether. As they wrestled, he heard the local train approaching in the tunnel behind him. It was the train for which he had been waiting. Mackay felt himself sliding toward the edge of the platform. Braced against an advertising poster, the gray-haired man was kicking at his legs, trying to hook and trip him. Mackay fought for his life.

As the local pulled into the station, the man tried to shove Mackay against it. When the doors opened, people hurried past them, getting on the train or off it. For a moment he caught a glimpse of the old woman he had thought to protect. She was inside the train now, watching through the window with a disapproving frown. Then he had to turn his head away to keep the madman's fingers out of his eyes.

Aware of the unheeding crowd, Mackay felt bound all the deeper in his dreaming state. In one of his recurring dreams, he would always find himself alone in a crowd, a foreign unregarded presence, the representative of Otherness. At the height of the nightmare some guilty secret or possession of his would be exposed to the crowd and draw their pitiless alien laughter.

The local gathered speed and pulled away. Mackay began to feel his strength ebbing, subverted by guilt, by weakness, by fear and indecision and lack of confidence. Somewhere in the darkness the next express was on its way. With his back to the tracks, Mackay held on.

They fell together to the filthy platform and rolled over, struggling in the half-light. The platform was deserted now. Distant voices echoed in tiled corridors. Mackay's assailant struggled to his feet and began to kick him. Mackay tried to dodge away; he was caught and kicked. Unable to escape, he dove at the man's legs and brought him down.

Again they rolled across the platform. Mackay took hold of the other man's hair and tried to ram his head against a steel pillar. The man butted him, breaking teeth, bloodying his mouth. Struggling to his feet, Mackay turned to run, but feeling the man's grip, turned to face him. He knew that was better than turning his back. The tunnel rang with the screech and roar of another train, bearing down on the express track.

Mackay took hold of his assailant's jacket and tried to bind him in the cloth. The man broke free and got an arm around Mackay's neck. The man's body had an evil smell. Driven by terror, Mackay somehow broke the hold and they were face to face again and literally hand to hand. The lunatic was pushing forward. He seized Mackay's arms at the biceps, trying to gather strength for the shove that would impel him off the platform.

Freeing his right arm, Mackay landed a lucky punch that brought his knuckles hard against the older man's collarbone. The man raised both hands to protect his throat. Explosively, an empty darkened train roared out of the tunnel and along the express track, passing through the station without stopping.

With his arms free, Mackay hurled punch after punch in panic and desperation. He heard, or thought that he heard, bone crack and felt the contours of his opponent's face yield to his fists. Sensing indecision in the older man's movements, he was driven to a blind fury, swinging hard and wild until his arms hung useless at his sides. Many hours later, when both his hands seemed to have swollen to the size of outfielders' gloves, he would discover that he had sustained multiple fractures in both hands.

Pale-faced and vacant-eyed, the strange German sat down on the platform and shouted. It took Mackay several seconds to realize that the man was shouting for help.

"Help!" the man called at the top of his voice. "Help me someone please!"

Mackay leaned against a signboard, breathing with difficulty. He was so tired that he was afraid of losing consciousness. His vision seemed peculiar; it was as if he saw the dim empty station around him in spasms of perception, framed in separated fragments of time. The disconnectedness of things, he saw, was fundamental. Years later, photographing a civil war in Nigeria, he would find the scenes of combat strangely familiar. The mode of perception discovered in the course of his absurd subway battle would serve him well. He would go where the wars and mobs were, photographing bad history in fragmented time. He had the eye.

At his feet, a bleeding man sat shouting for help. Mackay moved panting toward the subway stairs. There was blood on his hands. When he reached the foot of the stairs, he saw for the first time that the stairway was crowded with people and that many of the people were shouting as well. At first he could make no sense of it.

Then it came to him that the people on the stairs had come down and seen him beating a well-dressed older man. Mackay was wearing his navy peacoat, which was too warm for the weather, and his painting clothes. It was March 1965, and his hair hung down halfway to his shoulders. He had grown a beard from the first of the year. The people had been afraid to come down to the platform.

"Police!" someone shouted. "Call the police!"

Mackay remembered the mounted policeman bearing down on him in the park years before. His impulse was toward flight. He imagined a summoned policeman coming down the stairs. He imagined his own panic-stricken flight to the dead end of the platform. He saw himself shot down.

Burning with fear and outrage, Mackay hurled himself up the stairway and shoved his way, bloody-handed, through the crowd. The people nearest him snarled in terror as he passed.

"Police!" someone else shouted. Mackay shook off a hand on his arm. Someone punched him from behind. The crowd seemed monstrous, like the mob in a Brueghel crucifixion. A driven creature, with fists and elbows, he cut his way up to the light.

Headlong into the intersection Mackay ran. Cars swerved and skidded to a halt around him. Scattering pensioners and pigeons in Verdi Square, he kept on, faster and faster, increasing speed with every block. For neither the first nor the last time then, he wondered just how far he would run and where it was that he thought to go.

PORQUE NO TIENE, PORQUE LE FALTA

➤

La Cucaracha, La Cucaracha,
Ya no puede caminar
Porque no tiene, porque le falta
Marijuana par' fumar.
— A song of the revolution

THE WORDS came on the wind, an old woman's voice.
"Ayeee! Es-cor-pee-o-nays!"

He was lying in a smelly hammock under the concrete veranda with a thermos jug of Coke and alcohol balanced on his bare belly; when he understood the words he raised his head and pushed back the brim of his baseball cap.

"Escorpiónes!"

His children were running through the dry brush between his house and the beach. In the fiery sunlight their speeding forms were brown blurs topped with the flax of sun-bleached hair. He saw at once that they had not been bitten.

Doña Laura, the landlady, was calling to them from the roof of her house, where she had been hanging out black and white washing, warning them of the dangers of the brush. Doña Laura lived in fear of scorpions. She had lived among scorpions all her life and never been stung. Twice an hour she warned Richard and Jane away from them.

"No, no, no, no," Doña Laura shouted. *"Escorpiónes!"*

He could picture the word in her mouth, shaped on the dry lips, shrilled from strained corded muscles in a brown throat.

Escorpiónes.

The day was clear and the mountains at all points of the bay glowed bright green, but far out to sea dark low clouds approached, discoloring the surface of the distant ocean. Before long there would be heat lightning and rain. He took a drink from the thermos, closed his eyes and shuddered. Swallowing made the sweat on his chest run cold.

His children shouted, safe on the dry white sand.

The changing color of the sea made him uneasy. In the past months he had developed an odd passion for constancy; he liked things to stay as they were. When it was light he did not want it to grow dark, in spite of the beauty of the ocean sunset, and when it was dark he did not care for dawn to come and reveal his existence and position. But the time of year for constancy had passed and he was learning to live with the rains.

As he watched the clouds darken the reefs beyond the bay, a blue shape rose furiously from the clear unclouded shallows and slapped over the surface like a flung slate toward the darker waters. He could see the winged shadow it cast.

He sat up, straddling the hammock, and squinted after it.

"Marge," he called out.

After a moment his wife came out and stood beside him. She had pinned her light hair back behind her ears; the strands of hair on her neck were wet with perspiration. The white bikini she had made from a sheet was pasted to the curves of her body. There was tortilla dough on her hands.

"There's a manta off Guardia rock."

It seemed to take her a moment to understand. She turned slowly toward the bay with a faint polite smile and leaned forward over the patio wall, resting her elbows on the tile.

He watched her while she watched the water: she was alert from the shoulders forward; the rest of her body was lazily distributed in a balanced sprawl as though she had tossed it behind her. He had taken to observing her dynamics since she had caught the plague, in the course of which disorder her belly had become swollen and her long limbs wasted and spare. She and both of the children had suffered from the same disease — it was a variety of the local dysentery — and in its grip Marge and Jane and Richard had each commenced to dwindle away. Upon recovery, their flesh returned, and he had watched his wife regain the natural opulence of her body with dispassionate satisfaction. It was a visual diversion.

"Sure as shit," Marge said.

She had seen the creature rise.

Fletch considered Marge's response with distaste. It was a drag the way everyone had come to talk like a cowboy. Everyone called each other "hoss" and chuckled "haw haw," country style. Goldang. It was Fencer's influence. Fencer was a cowboy number.

"Fencer saw a manta ray while he was out swimming," Marge said. "He was out by the rocks when he saw this big mother coming at him about twenty yards away. Started swimming for it with the wingspread bearing down on him. He says it was like the manta was trying to embrace him. A love trip, you know? Like this big slime thing was consumed with affection for Fencer and wanted to wrap him up and take him home. Fencer had his air gun. He says that would have been sad to have gut shot the thing and watch its poor fish face wrinkle up all disillusioned and die."

"Fencer can't possibly swim faster than a ray," Fletch told her.

"What would it do if it caught you?" Marge asked. "Flap you to death? Butt you? Eat you?"

"We'll find out when one catches Fencer," Fletch said.

"Hey now, where are they?" She meant the children. She had caught their voices and cocked an ear to the wind.

"They're on the beach. Doña Laura's watching them."

The bay had gone dark; the clouds came overhead, heavy with rain. Heat lightning flashed out to sea. On the north headland, Fletch could see the villa where Sinister Pancho Pillow lived etched in the sky's sickly light; the hillside against which it stood had turned dark green.

Fletch became unhappy. He reached under the hammock, took his makings from a cedar box and began to roll a joint. Marge sat down beside him and for a few minutes they turned on and watched the storm gather. Marge drummed on her thighs, leaving a film of flour on the tanned skin.

"Fencer's coming, you know," Marge said.

Fletch extinguished the joint and lay sidewise on the hammock with his head beside the swell of Marge's hip.

"Why?"

Marge looked down at him, blank-eyed.

"Well, to take you up to the volcano. You said you wanted to see it. He wants to take you."

"I never said I wanted to see the volcano. I mean, I can see it from here." The volcano was behind them, rising from the sierra. Fletch did not turn toward it.

"Fencer asked you just the other day. You said you wanted to go very much."

"No such conversation took place," Fletch told her.

The rain seemed to hang back. They sat in silence watching the clouds until they heard a car turn off the coast road. Fletch waited motionless until Fencer's '49 Buick rolled up before the house.

Fencer was in the front seat beside Willie Wings; he was smiling happily at them, dangling one bare arm along the dusty surface of the car door. Fencer's Buick was painted with thick blue and gold loops like the stylized waves of a Hokusai seascape.

"I don't want to see the fucking volcano," Fletch said.

"I bet you go," Marge told him.

Fencer and Willie Wings got out and walked toward them. Fencer was wearing his white duck pirate pants and his Pima Indian necklace with a Maltese cross soldered to the chain. He wore his yellow hair like General Custer.

Willie Wings shuffled along beside him carrying a parrot in a cage. Breathless from the morning's methedrine, he was addressing the bird. His face and the bald crown of his head were red and sweaty.

"Look at Fletch, Godfrey," Willie Wings enjoined the parrot. "You see Fletch over there?"

Fletch turned away and lowered the brim of his cap over his eyes. He felt colder at that moment than he had ever felt in Mexico.

"It's a good day," Fencer declared, striking a posture before them. "Here we are and Willie Wings has his parrot."

"Can you say 'Fletch'?" Willie Wings asked the parrot. "Say 'Come see the volcano, Fletch.'"

"Willie's been tryin' to train Godfrey to sit on his shoulder," Fencer said, "but it don't never work. So he just carries him around."

Willie Wings scratched at his denims with a free hand and shook the cage.

"Godfrey's literary, that's what his trouble is. I'm not saying he's verbal but he's literary. He's like Fletch."

Willie's clear gaze swept the scene. Fletch remained under his hat.

"Godfrey and Fletch and Mrs. Fletch are all literary and that's a handicap." Willie turned from them, marched away ten steps, wheeled and approached talking.

"Which isn't to say I don't have my own literary side except I haven't got the technical training in Paris and Bucharest of higher poetics before the crowned heads of Europe which is what Godfrey and Fletch and Marge think they have over me."

He stopped and smiled on his parrot with broken teeth.

"Oh you doll, Godfrey! You pseudo-intellectual."

"We got beer in the car," Fencer said. "Let's have a beer, Willie Wings."

Willie set the parrot down and went to the car to wrestle the beer from the trunk.

"Willie had another bad scene with that Chinaman grocer," Fencer said as they watched him. "Pretty soon ol' Hong won't sell us no more beer."

Marge shook her head.

"I thought you took his crystal, Fencer," she said. "He's really too much now and then."

Fencer looked sad.

"Willie gave up crystal. He handed me what he had and made me swear I'd only give him what he really needed. But he got some more somewhere and he's shooting it again. I think maybe he got it from Sinister Pancho Pillow."

"His mind is running off its reel," Fletch said. "He's going to end up in a speed museum."

"I got a deep personal esteem for Willie Wings," Fencer told them. "My friends don't appreciate that. He's an avatar."

Fletch said nothing.

"Well he's certainly a very good driver," Marge said.

"He's a lot more than that," Fencer said. "Aw, just look at him with animals."

Fletch savored the imaginary cold under his hat brim. He considered Willie Wings's relationship to animals and Fencer's relationship to Willie Wings.

"Remember Willie's dog?" Fencer asked. His eyes sparkled with humorous affection. "Remember Ol' Crush?"

Marge laughed, joining in the mood of nostalgia. "Oh, God," she cried, "Ol' Crush."

Fletch recalled the days when Willie's mind had been clearer and he had been a dealer in the Haight. He had maintained a

German shepherd named Old Crush, although according to Willie it was an Alsatian and had been trained to kill in French. Willie, in those days, had been more political and would have no traffic with German killer dogs; Old Crush had been raised by anti-fascists, and attacked at the command *"Mort aux vaches."*

When a deal was consummated Willie Wings and the customer would turn on together, and when everyone was suitably high Willie would introduce Old Crush from an adjoining room.

"Don't betray the slightest sign of fear," Willie would advise his guests, "or he'll tear you to pieces."

Willie Wings set the case of beer down on the patio and stood before them panting.

"I hear you had more trouble with Mr. Hong," Marge inquired.

Willie rolled his eyes. "Don't think Orientals can't sense dharma strength," he said. "When Hong sold me that beer, we lived out the Eon of the Void together, and he fought me every step of the way." He picked up the caged parrot and shook it. "Didn't he, Godfrey?"

"Hong is afraid of you," Marge explained, "because he thinks you're crazy. He's afraid of Fencer, too."

"That reminds me," Willie Wings said. "Let's go see the volcano. Let's take Fletch."

"That's why we're here," Fencer said. "Let's go, Fletch."

The rain broke suddenly. Fletch sat silently, listened to it for a while, and lifted his hat.

"Well," he said, sitting up, "I do want to go up there and see it."

"Yeah, yeah, yeah," Willie Wings sang. "There are fire flowers up there, Fletch. Along the rim. Black rock and fire flowers."

"But . . . I don't think I want to go today."

Willie Wings stared at Fletch in horror.

"I don't like it, Fencer," he said. "I didn't like it before and I don't like it now." He looked at Marge and Fletch in turn. "Why not? I don't understand. What is this, some kind of literary mood? Some kind of balky bolting? Some kind of not doing what the guys have come to do?"

"This would be the best time to go," Fencer said.

"It isn't that I don't want to see the thing," Fletch explained, "because I certainly do . . ."

He made what seemed to him an intense effort to conclude his statement but found himself unable to do so.

"Well, good," Fencer said. "Let's go, hoss. Let's have a joint and go."

Fencer had the joints under his belt. He produced them with astounding grace and speed; they shot from hand to hand like flaming arrows. Fletch took his tokes one after another, feeling that it was somehow against his will. It occurred to him that he did not have to go with Fencer and Willie Wings to the volcano but that he was very high.

"That's all I want," he said after a while.

"Too much," Willie Wings cried.

They all had another joint and washed the grass sediment down with cold beer.

"I lust after that mountain," Fencer said. "I've got to get up there."

The rain stopped. Within seconds the wet leaves of the vanilla trees beside the patio were drying.

"Marge," Fletch said, "do you want to go?"

"No," she said.

Fencer and Willie Wings watched her.

"Why not?"

"I'll stay down here with the kids. I have to."

She leaned against the wall. A small lizard ran between her sandaled feet.

Fletch stood up and looked at the ocean.

"If I had said I was going," Marge told him, "and Fencer and Willie Wings had come to take me, I would go."

"Right," Fletch said.

"Man," Fencer said, "we've got to get up there. We've got to leave now while it's light."

"Right," Fletch said. He picked up the thermos of Coke and alcohol and walked to the car. He felt curiously cold in the sunlight.

The inside of Fencer's car was stifling. Fletch sat down between a tire and some empty gasoline cans. The car smelled of gasoline and the steaming rotten upholstery.

Fencer and Willie got in. As the car pulled away, Fletch watched his wife go inside and close the door.

"When we get up there, Fletch," Fencer said, "you'll see it's a great place for a poet. Then I won't have to describe it for you anymore."

"When Fletch sees it," Willie Wings said, "he can describe it for us. Because being a poet he can describe things better than we can."

He turned around to face Fletch.

"Fletch has had too many things described to him. It's time he had something of his own to describe."

Fletch looked out the window at the rows of banana trees.

"Who is he talking about, Fencer? Is he really talking about me?"

"You know that better than I do, Fletch," Fencer said. "Sounds like he is."

They drove along the coast highway between the plantations and the beach. Just outside the village, where the police post was, the Indians were lined along the road in their Sunday suits, holding palm fronds and flags. Five men in silver-studded vests stood behind the crowd with instruments at the ready — two trumpeters, a tuba player, a drummer and a cymbalist. People in the crowd held lengths of a banner reading BIENVENIDOS PADRE URRIETA!

Fencer and Willie Wings saluted the crowd as they drove by. Fencer salaamed and Willie Wings, his fingers joined to suggest the Trinity, dispensed papal benedictions.

"*Diablo,*" someone shouted.

Fletch crouched down beside the tire in a position from which he could see only the crests of palm trees and the sky.

After a while they turned inland, following the straight plantation roads through armies of coconut palm. At the turn where the road curved upward into the sierra, they started a covey of vultures from the jungle. The birds flapped about the car windows in alarm.

"Hong won't sell me tarot cards," Willie Wings said. "He told me no, absolutely refused to sell me them, won't have me near them."

"He probably doesn't have tarot cards," Fletch said. "He's a grocer."

"I know what Hong has," Willie said heatedly. "I know everything about him." Willie was popping pills; he turned to Fencer in a fury. "Listen, Fencer, how can he be a poet? He don't live the conscious life. He lives unawares."

"You reckon there's truth in that?" Fencer asked.

"No," Fletch said. "I live the conscious life."

Fencer smiled at him in the rear-view mirror.

"You hear that, Fencer?" Willie Wings shouted. "You hear what he said?"

Fletch stared at the moist flushed surface of Willie's head and felt a thrill of fear.

"Everyone has a potential level of consciousness," Fencer said kindly. "There's a vein of deep perception in all beings. The thing is to bring it out."

"Fletch's perception is dead," Willie Wings declared. He began to assemble a joint of his own. "Like a dead nerve in a tooth."

They were leaving the low ground. Palms gave way to occasional live oak, Spanish cedar and euphorbia; vines covered the road. They ascended a green spiral, and at the turns Fletch could see the bay below.

He said nothing, but when Willie Wings presented the next joint he accepted it. His perception, he reminded himself, was not dead but throbbed within his lax and ill-used body, a secret agent. Crouched low in the back seat, he stared dully toward the mass of the sierra and tried to consider the action.

They were taking him up to the volcano. When the moment came, he promised himself, he would act appropriately.

The smell of thick-fleshed green things was suffocating. The wind that resisted their climb was heavy and sweet.

"I was once the only white bellhop in Chattanooga," Willie Wings told them when the joint had been consumed. "Years and years ago at the start of my career. I worked in an eight-story hotel. You see me, right? Youthful in those days, with glossy black hair that indicated my Cherokee blood. Braided uniform, kind of like the staff drape at the Hotel Dixie on Forty-two Street when the bus depot was up there. Only it's an eight-story hotel in Chattanooga — take it off the stationery.

"Now I couldn't begin to lay on you the parts of the human heart I witnessed there. Forget the microcosm — it was more than that. Eight stories high.

"You *know*, don't you, that I saw lots of shit to appeal to the prurient interest? I saw every variety of sexuality known to the Eastern masters. Dig it! In each and every room was a viewee thing — sometimes it was a little hole, sometimes it was more complicated, because this was in the great age of hotels."

Fletch listened with growing panic. While Willie Wings paused to do a speed item, he raised his thermos and drank. He tried to do so in absolute silence, and huddled even lower in the seat so that he would not be seen. Willie caught him all the same.

"Fencer!" Willie cried, so loudly that the bird beside him set up a squawk in anxious imitation. "Look at Fletch with that lush! Look at him suck on it."

Fencer smiled tolerantly. "Fletch is just relaxing."

"Don't get so juiced I can't tell you, Fletch — I'm talking about Chattanooga! I'm talking about that eight-story hotel!" He raised his clenched hand as though he were wrestling with angels.

"Every notion that could be acted upon with the human body was acted upon under my eyes, baby. My nights were rich — they were cloying. But — listen to this, Fletch — of all those fleshy games I saw played, the most spectacular beyond any shadow of a doubt was played by one man! One solitary, ordinary-looking citizen in a room by himself! I have never again seen anything like it."

Willie Wings paused to catch his breath. He rubbed his hands together.

"So . . ." he sighed, and a drawling self-deprecation came into his voice, "so waal you could say it was just a cat playing with himself." He leaned his head on the seat as though overcome. "But let me tell you," he said softly, "let me tell you, buddies — he *really* played with himself."

When Willie Wings settled back, exhausted, Fletch saw that his eyes were filled with tears.

Fencer was flushed with affection. When he spoke it was with difficulty. "Oh God, Willie. Oh, Willie."

Willie Wings sat with eyes closed, nodding.

"Oh, Willie," Fencer said.

"Yeah," Willie said. "Yeah, yeah, yeah."

Fencer sought Fletch in the rear-view mirror.

"Fletch," he said gently, "can't you get with us?"

"Jesus Christ," Fletch said. He said it quite involuntarily.

Willie Wings, his reverie shattered, turned and glared.

"I'm sorry I told you, Fletch, you're such a drag. I'm really pissed now," he told Fencer, "and I'm a little sorry about what's happening."

"Don't be," Fencer said reassuringly. "Don't regret nothing."

On the leeward side of the mountains, the land was much drier. Jungle clung to the canyons, but there were broad expanses of brushland grown with mesquite and agave and flowering redbird cactus. Occasionally the road ran past shapeless masses of concrete where half-finished constructions had been trapped by floods from the rain-soaked sierra and left to molder.

Whenever a burro or a longhorn cow went by, Willie Wings, who loved animals, had a good word to say for it.

Fletch rested his head on the tire in a state of deep depression. From time to time, he would attempt to bring himself up with a drink from his thermos, but to no avail. They were, he had noted, only a few kilometers from Corbera, the highest town in the valley — from there the road climbed steadily toward the dirt track that led to the crater. If he was to get out of the car and have no more of Fencer and Willie Wings he would have to do it in Corbera, from where a bus ran to the coast. If he flung himself out of the car, as he now and then considered, they would simply stop and come back for him and he would have to explain to Willie Wings.

Corbera was about ten minutes away; one drove through it completely in five minutes — he had therefore only fifteen minutes to devise a ruse or a confusion in which he might make his escape.

He lay back and considered his prospects — Willie and Fencer had fallen silent. They passed the Purina plant which marked the outskirts of Corbera. Fourteen minutes. Fletch took another drink; the parrot squawked to alert Willie Wings. Thirteen minutes.

Fletch considered the peculiar question of whether there had ever been an element of choice connected with his excursion. One thing was certain: he had not refused to come. He thought this significant.

At the moment when his rational process was most acutely engaged, his thoughts were frighted by the hated voice of Willie Wings.

"Now that man in Chattanooga didn't claim to be no poet," Willie told him. "But all by himself in that there hotel room *he wailed*. He set his consciousness on fire! That was life I was witnessing, Fletch, at my peephole. So when I meet guys like you . . ."

Fletch stared wide-eyed at the telegraph wires outside. Twelve minutes . . . Eleven minutes.

Willie Wings had raised both arms above his head like a bouzouki dancer and was waggling his thick fingers over the reddened dome of his head.

"Then I think, Wow, man, how groovy it is to be human! What a beautiful thing to be alive and conscious. And I think of that summer night in the shadow of Lookout Mountain — the cat on his own self and me on my peephole — the two of us there, human and conscious, the perceiver and the perceived, man, and I think that's the most beautiful night of my life spiritually."

He turned to look at Fletch, but seeing only the rear window he cried out in alarm. "Fencer! Where's Fletch?"

Fletch had sunk to the floor and was gripping the tire with both hands.

"Fletch!" Willie called and leaned over the seat to discover him. "You once-born emptiness, you better hide." He bent himself double over the back to shout in Fletch's ear. "In spite of you, man, the world is rich!"

Fletch twisted on the thought. He pulled himself upright and took a drink.

Fencer watched him in the mirror. "Stay in it, Fletch. Everything's gonna be groovy."

"You fucking repulsive baldheaded rat," Fletch said to Willie. "Who wants to hear about your lousy life?"

Willie Wings stared in astonishment.

Fencer looked concerned.

"Don't be an asshole," he cautioned Fletch. "Don't overreact."

The world is rich in spite of me, Fletch thought furiously.

"You creepy bastards! All I know is creepy bastards!" Fletch could not contain himself. "My life is poisoned!"

Willie Wings recovered himself.

"Nobody sounds me," he declared violently. "No literary poet abuses me! It's love me — love my thing! I got my own thing, Fencer. I got friends that love me and revere me and protect me from the literary poets that want to destroy me because the literary poets have always wanted to destroy me. I don't know how many times I been bum-tripped and burned by poets and I hate the bastards!"

"You . . ." Fletch began.

"You think I can't protect myself from you?" Willie shouted. "You think I'm defenseless?" He laughed derangedly. "I got a hard desperate side for my own protection," he told them. "I got a piece!" He began to claw at the inside of his leg, which was where he strapped his pistol.

"Yeah," Willie Wings said. His eyes were fixed as though confronting some inevitability; his hand was on the concealed holster.

Fencer began to slap at him blindly with his free arm.

"Willie, Willie, that ain't the way."

"Whaddaya mean it ain't the way, Fencer? What's the way then?"

"The way," Fencer said, "is to go up the mountain and make it all complete." He sought Fletch in the mirror again. "Right, Fletch?"

Fletch stared glassy-eyed at the bulge along Willie's calf where the gun was.

"Let me out," he said dully. "I get out here."

They were in the *zócalo* of Corbera. On the left Fletch saw the veranda of the Hotel Volcánico, on the right the Azteca Cinema was playing *Sangre y Plata* with Errol Flynn.

"No," Fencer said. "We got to finish it."

Willie Wings had regained his composure. "I'll go along with that," he said. "Fletch stays."

There was a wall of peanuts on the north end of the square where the vendors had set up their stalls outside the municipal market. Fletch was suddenly inspired. He thrust himself over the seat and seized the wheel. Fencer hung on and decelerated.

"Let me out," Fletch told him. "I'll run us on the peanuts."

A vendor approached them with a basketful of nuts.

"*Cacahuetes*," he moaned. "*Cacahuetes?*"

Fencer and Willie Wings sat in silent fury.

Fletch gathered up his thermos and prepared to alight. He was trembling.

"*Cacahuetes*," sang the peanut vendor.

Without warning, Fencer rammed into gear. Fletch saw the market fall away in a spray of peanuts as he flew into the back seat.

"*Gringo!*" the stricken peanut man called after them. "*Gringo!*"

Fletch floundered in the seat. His trousers were soaked in Coke and alcohol.

"Take it easy, Fletch," Fencer said earnestly. "Show him, Willie."

"Don't panic, Fletch," Willie said. "But the Sinister Pancho

Pillow was just pulling up behind us." He pointed tensely through the rear window.

About thirty yards behind them was a new Lincoln with California plates. The driver, barely visible, was a fat, dark-skinned man who wore a goatee and dark glasses. A girl in a straw hat sat beside him, and there was a third person in the back.

Fletch stared at them.

"Well there it is, Fletch," Fencer said. "You panicked. You balked. And you nearly set us up for Sinister Pancho Pillow."

"And his woman, La Beatriz," Willie Wings said.

"And La Beatriz. And Pancho's Odd Buddy." Fencer whistled through his teeth. "Don't that show you somethin' about how the world is set up, Fletch? There you were, acting like me and Willie Wings was a menace, and in the next fuckin' instant Sinister Pancho Pillow makes the scene."

Fletch thought of prayer. He addressed a prayer to his perception, which he felt was in danger of obliteration, together with its frail equipage. He beseeched his perception to overcome panic and confusion.

"I have nothing to fear from Pancho Pillow," he told them. "What do I care if he pulls up behind us?"

"Let us not leave those evils which we got," Willie Wings said, "and flee to others which we know not of."

Fencer nodded vigorously. "That's a relevant quote, Fletch. Hey, man, are they still behind us?"

"They turned off," Fletch said. "They're going back to the coast."

"That's a feint," Fencer said. "They're gonna stay out there behind us somewhere."

The sloping plains they drove through were bare, although patches of cypress forest rose in the barrancas below them.

They were above Corbera now. Ahead the road ran quite literally to the clouds.

Fencer was rolling a joint while driving. He was one of the few people in Mexico who could do so. Fletch watched him jab the lighted end toward Willie with an impatient gesture. That, Fletch thought, must be why they called him Fencer.

Fletch had resolved to turn on in order to buy time. If he accepted the new joint, it seemed to him that he would not get very much higher than he was. Moreover, the forms of order would be maintained, perception stimulated and panic postponed.

Fencer became philosophical. "Paranoids make their own hell," he told Fletch. "Here you were with just me and Willie and all aggressive and paranoid. Next thing — wham — it's Sinister Pancho Pillow time. Don't that make you think?"

"What's the matter with Pancho Pillow?" Fletch asked. "I mean, compared with you and Willie Wings?"

"Nothin' wrong with Pancho for the average person," Willie said. "Plenty wrong for you though, Fletch — you better believe it. Because we're with you down deep, Fletch. But Sinister Pancho Pillow ain't with no one and he'd eat you up."

"Why?" Fletch asked.

"Why?" Willie Wings sighed. "Because you're his favorite flavor."

Fletch affected to laugh.

"Oh now this is really a lot of shit," he said.

Willie looked at him kindly.

"That really is a lot of shit," Fletch told them. "It's utter jive. You're crazy with speed, all of you."

"I'm afraid Willie's right, Fletch," Fencer said. "But we're all in the same bag, children, because Sinister Pancho Pillow has hunger and thirst for all of us."

"Not for me," Willie Wings said. He rattled the parrot's cage, making the bird squawk.

"Especially for you, Willie Wings," Fencer said. "Sorry."

Fletch shook his head.

"Oh now this really is a lot of shit," he said.

"Too bad you can't make your own world," Fencer said. "But you got to live the world the way it is, I hate to tell you. If I made the world and the firmament, I wouldn't have no Pancho Pillows in it. But there he is, Virginia, sorry about that."

"Now this . . ." Fletch began.

"If Pancho had come on us back in Corbera," Fencer went on, "he'd have wanted into your life. If he'd seen we was all together — and that Willie Wings was around — he'd have been just overjoyed. He'd have suggested a picnic."

"And you'd have been sorry quick," Willie Wings added. Willie had turned morose.

"Pancho's a body snatcher," Fencer told them. "That's my theory. A body snatcher and an agent and one of the world's worst bummers."

"He's been known to wear a badge," Willie said. "He showed a friend of mine one once."

"Sure as shit," Fencer said. "I've seen him appear on the border and the score went bad. I know for a fact he was around that bad Lee Oswald fella in Mex City. When Miss Liz Taylor lost something up in P.V., they went to Pancho Pillow to get it back."

"You want to freak the cats in Mexicali?" Willie Wings asked Fletch. "Bop over to the One-Eyed Indian Bar and tell them 'Pancho Pillow's in town!' Man, you'll dig them choke and turn gray and their knees'll knock together. That's what they think of Panch in Mexicali."

"Fuck him, is all," Fencer said. "Forget him. Let's go see the volcano."

They drove over a plateau surrounded by brown peaks. The wind had a taste Fletch had forgotten. It was late in the day; the light was fading in the sky and the peaks cast long conical shadows over the dun sand.

They came to the dirt track. Fencer eased the car off the

highway and followed it. The track ran in shadow and Fletch was aware of the mass of the volcano rising above them. Bursts of smoke came at the windshield like yellow flak.

Fletch watched Willie and Fencer in the peculiar light.

"I dig the high windies, man," Fencer said. "I love it up here."

There was no life to be seen. Not even goats grazed on the sulfurous pasture. There were no bird calls, not even a buzzard in the sky. The smoke grew thicker.

"Hang in, Fletch," Fencer said. "We get out in half a mile."

Their faces were caked with dust. Willie's parrot had begun to make faint cooing noises.

Fletch turned in his seat and looked with longing at the descending track behind them.

"Maybe," he said at length, "maybe . . . we could come to an understanding."

Fencer smiled. "That's what we're up here for."

"I didn't really have to come up," Fletch told them, "but as it is, I did. I could have avoided this. There was plenty of places I could have gotten out — I almost did get out, didn't I? There were plenty of reasons. But, as it is, I stayed in all the way."

Fencer nodded. Willie began to hum "The Streets of Laredo."

"So if I came all this way, it shows some willingness, doesn't it? It shows some . . ." He paused and looked uneasily at the sky. "It shows some trust — how about that?"

The road ended in a depression of ocher mud veined with cracks. A wall of black volcanic rock faced them, rising toward the peak and sloping downward toward iron-toothed canyons which they could not see. The wind carried only silence.

"If a man like me can show so much trust to you and Willie Wings, it shows we've got something going together, right?"

"Don't try to verbalize it," Fencer said. "You'll just fuck it up."

They got out of the car and stood before a sign that pointed straight upward. The sign said that San Isobel was five kilometers away; it was riddled with bullet holes.

"If we've got this much going," Fletch told them, "we don't have to go through with any kind of stunts, do we, Fencer? We don't have to have sentimental dramas to act out where we're at."

Fencer and Willie looked at him sympathetically.

"I mean, we're all party to the same thing. I proved that by coming up here."

"You're sure party to something, Fletch," Fencer agreed. "But see, we've got to go up on the volcano."

"Literary Fletch," Willie Wings said.

The path they were to follow led over the rock at the edge of the mountainside. There was no path leading downward.

"It's gonna be dark," Fencer said. "That'll make it harder."

Fletch saw that they were waiting for him to lead.

He took a drink from the thermos and stepped forward.

"Maybe," he said, "we could all begin again."

When he closed his eyes, he saw the formless colors of the mountain. Yellow and black. He tried to raise the thermos again but failed to muster the strength. Opening his eyes, he looked at the steep path for a moment. Then he raised the thermos and hurled it, with surprising force, into Willie's face.

Ax edges of rock flew up at him as he leaped; the merciless ground tore at his shoes. At times it seemed to him that he was bouncing, gliding over clefts and boulders like a hurdler. He could hear the parrot squawking and Fencer shouting "No!" Once he turned and saw Fencer start after him.

Willie had climbed on a rock and was screaming, waving his pistol. "Don't you play gingerbread boy with me, you fuckin' poet!"

Fencer had stopped and was shouting "No!" at Willie. Fletch

heard a pistol shot and somewhere a bullet rang against the iron-fibered rock.

When he heard the car engine start up, he ran faster. It was all down, over rank after rank of jagged rock.

After a while, he found the dry bed of a stream and followed it through a dark arroyo. The farther down he went, the more difficult it became for him to see; shadow and rock grew together. After about a mile he could no longer run because the ground was too steep — he climbed downward, facing the rock wall. His knees were bloody but his feet found holds with a sure instinct. At one point a cloud passed over him, leaving him chilled through, and when the cloud had passed he saw that night was coming on the valley below. He could see the last of sunlight play on green waxy leaf in the fingers of rain forest along the lower slope. He found a stretch of smoother rock on which to rest and let the night slip over him. Sounds of a life he had not suspected rustled from the barren ground.

Leaning back against the rock, he tried to shake the colors of the day from his mind. After a while, he discovered the remnant of a joint in his trouser pocket and, having no matches, ate it. The shadows of the valley swayed beneath his feet. In the distance he could see the lights of Corbera, the illumination of the cathedral tower and the wooden bullring.

He began to regret that he had not seen the crater. He deserved to see it, it seemed to him, since he had come all the way and crowned the journey with a masterly escape. Willie Wings and Fencer had sealed him in a box of speed madness that interfered with the spontaneous joys of active living — they were mere circumstances, artifacts. Yet it had been necessary to escape them: the pair were overripe, deracinated by years of smoking grass in the tropics, consumed by maniac ravings and heaven knew what bizarre commitments to serpent-headed lava gods and human sacrifice.

It was humiliating, he thought, to be forced to survive by guile, but in a crisis, could he not bring it to bear? Indeed, it seemed to him, he could.

As the world darkened, Fletch became more and more exhilarated, and for a time he considered retracing his steps and going to the crater after all. But he stayed where he was until the moon rose and then stood up to survey the valley. As he watched, the lights of Corbera suddenly flickered and died — in a few seconds they went on, stayed on for a short time, and died again. Fletch stood waiting, saw the lights return, flicker, disappear. He found the spectacle intensely gratifying. Corbera was a light show.

Heat lightning was flashing over the coast range. Fletch stretched out his arms and with Jovian fingers began to play the illuminations one against the other — with one hand he dispensed lightning for the firmament, with the other darkness for the sons of men. The lightning and the town's electricity followed the bidding of his fingers with precision.

Fletch cried out joyfully from his Promethean rock.

"I'll be screwed if I'm not stout Cortés," he said.

Fletch became, in effect, stout Cortés. When the moon was high enough for him to see his way, he clambered downward, completely unafraid. The fer-de-lance slithering among the rocks, the lurking Gila monsters, the tigers in their caves were fine with him. At intervals he rested, looked up at the peak and saw dark vapors visible against the stars, against Taurus.

I'm all perception, Fletch thought as he descended, all I require is to be left alone by the likes of Fencer and Willie Wings. Revolting to be pursued by epiphenomena.

I am a fortress beset by flying men, he thought. The sleep of reason produces monsters.

Halfway down the slope, he found a trail and followed it; he could smell jungle and black earth below him. In a few minutes he had entered the forest. His passage set off a scurrying among the trees, a sudden silence broken by monkey cries, the din of cicadas and cinches. He felt his presence electrify the night.

"I am the sentient consciousness here," he said aloud.

He put his hand to a tree and felt hundreds of hard beetle bodies scurry along the surface of the vines. Every now and then lightning flashed above the trees, lighting the grove where he stood and leaving behind his eyes white lighted instants in which unknown creatures stood transfixed on the edge of vision.

Walking on, he found the downward slope still steep, and once, following what he thought to be a trail along a fallen tree trunk, he fell several feet onto soft earth, landed upright, scattering invisible creatures before him.

He walked for well over an hour with what he experienced as animal grace. When he came out of the woods, he found a dark shed beyond a wooden gate; open sewerage was somewhere near at hand. Continuing, he roused an enormous pig that grunted at him savagely — as he hurried on, pigs roused themselves in alarming numbers from the adjoining grounds. He found that he was atop a steep rise above the center of Corbera — the lights were on; he could hear music from the jukeboxes in the Calle Obregón.

The road was on the other side of the pig shed. Fletch followed it downhill toward the market, where intermittent paving and open street lights began.

He found the central square almost deserted. A few old Indian women selling beer dozed beside their stalls. Flags and tricolor pennants swung on the wind honoring the anniversary of the revolution.

The lights and the music were all on the Calle Obregón. Fletch made for it, walking tensely under the colonnades, expecting the lights to go at any moment. He kept his hands clenched to control his conductivity.

Calle Obregón was swarming with soldiery. Men in khaki uniforms were lined up in front of the cathouses drinking beer and clustered in the doorways of the open-fronted bars. Twenty jukeboxes sounded together.

Fletch went quickly. Two military policemen with carbines slung over their shoulders passed him with glances of grave suspicion.

The La Florida bar was where Fletch always went in Corbera. He admired the pastoral murals, which were true *art naïf,* and the section of earth floor around the bar. That night he found it crowded with cavalrymen, all drunk to the point of silence. He entered as quietly as possible and ordered a rum. As he drank it, a small boy approached with an electric shock machine.

The cavalryman nearest Fletch cursed softly, beckoned to the boy, and put fifty centavos in his hand. Then he gripped the metal handles, planting his feet firmly, legs apart, knees bent. Without looking at his customer, the boy turned the crank, and the soldier, his jaw set, his eyes half closed, received the current. The others watched him without expression. After a few seconds, the soldier's uniform shirt began to crackle and his hair to stand upon its roots. The machine glowed and the soldier's face twitched and his chin rose as though his head were being torn from his body. The boy turning the crank never glanced at him.

Fletch did not know very much about electricity but he admired the machine. The generator box was painted bright blue, and on it was the picture of a clenched fist emitting bolts of lightning, over the word *Corazón!* in pink letters. He suspected that the machine might be somehow involved in Corbera's fits of chiaroscuro.

The cavalryman had huge reserves of *Corazón!* and continued to hang on. Fletch took his drink to another electric spectacle, the jukebox in the back.

The jukebox, enormous and bright with shifting, laminated light, had scores of jungle moths fluttering around it. From time to time a moth would touch against the hot plastic surface and spin to the floor with singed wings. Around the foot of the box was a brilliant litter of burnt and dying moths.

Fletch had settled down in back when he saw Pancho Pillow seated at a nearby table. Pancho Pillow was smiling; he was accompanied by La Beatriz, who was also smiling, and by his Odd Buddy, who was not.

The sight of Pancho Pillow was so little suited to Fletch's mood that it took him a short time to remember that the strength of his perception had rendered him at peace with the world.

He carried his rum to Pancho's table.

"God save all here," he said.

The sight of Fletch seemed to send both Pancho Pillow and La Beatriz into spasms of delight. They laughed uproariously and La Beatriz pinched Pancho on the belly.

"Fletch!" Pancho cried. "Fletch, my friend to be! Sit down and drink with us."

Fletch sat down. La Beatriz affected to gaze on him with nymphic passion. Pancho's Odd Buddy watched the soldiers at the bar.

"I've been sad all day," Pancho said merrily. "We saw you today in the company of hoodlums." Pancho wore a brush mustache and had many chins. His light brown hair was combed straight up from his forehead. "We all wondered — what is a poet doing with hoodlums?" He made his little eyes twinkle confusion.

"That Fencer," La Beatriz said with distaste, "that Weelie Weengs! Eeee!" She flung her hand before Fletch's face as though she were trying to shake something off her fingers.

"I was taking the day off," Fletch said. "I woke up this morning and I said to myself, Today I'll do something less literary."

"You don't want to know Fencer and Willie Wings," Pancho

said. "They're bummers." He leaned forward and spoke softly. "My theory is they work with the body snatchers."

Fletch savored his drink.

"I have nothing to fear from Fencer and Willie Wings," he said. "They can't affect me in the essentials."

"Ah," Pancho said. "you can't cheat an honest man. Before W. C. Fields it was an Arab proverb, and you'd think the Arabs should know." He put his hand on Fletch's shoulder, then withdrew it. "But it's not true." He cupped his hands, turned them upside down and shrugged. "No, it's not true. My life hasn't been easy and I've cheated many honest men. It's just as untrue as it sounds."

Fletch laughed for quite a while. "What could they possibly cheat me out of?" he asked.

"What do Weelie Weengs and Fencer say about Pancho?" La Beatriz asked him. "They make up goodies on him?"

"Yes," Pancho said. "I was . . ." His hand fluttered in the air.

"You were too modest to ask," Fletch suggested.

Everyone laughed together.

"Well, actually, Pancho," Fletch said, pronouncing his auditor's name with difficulty, "they didn't say anything."

Pancho and La Beatriz hooted.

"Oh, come on, man," they said, in melodious unison.

Pancho Pillow's Odd Buddy turned to Fletch for the first time. Fletch saw that the two sides of his face did not match.

"They didn't tell you that one time me and Pancho drove from Belize to Jalapa with them in the trunk?"

Pancho intervened. "It was in a good cause," he assured Fletch.

Fletch drank his rum. He was content.

"I love Mexico," he told them. "You can take some fantastic rides here."

"What a poet!" Pancho Pillow exclaimed.

"Lord Byron," La Beatriz said.

The boy with the *Corazón!* machine approached and Pancho's Odd Buddy watched him eagerly, ogling the metal handles. He was reaching in his pocket for change when Pancho leaned forward to restrain him.

"Don't, Idaho," he said.

"What the hell," his Odd Buddy said protestingly.

"For me, Idaho," Pancho pleaded. "I don't want to watch."

The boy looked at them in disgust and went outside.

"You're in your element here, Fletch," Pancho said. "Not everyone is. Myself, I'm at home throughout the Spanish-speaking world."

Fletch nodded. "I am in my element here," he agreed. "That's true."

"I was born in Tunis," Pancho confided. "Hispano!" He breathed deeply and beat twice on his chest. "Superficially French in culture and outlook — a man of the world and a great traveler. But in the soul I'm Hispano, that's where it's at."

"Everyone should have a souly country," Fletch said.

"I admire simplicity of heart," Pancho said. "I despise hypocrisy and deceit, so I have no use for politics."

He looked at Fletch in admiration.

"I myself am poetical. My view of life, my way of looking at the world, is poetical. If I wasn't a businessman, that would be my groove." Pancho seemed to grow emotional.

"Listen to me, Fletch, we can use some poetry in our lives. Let's really get together — nothing superficial. I have a story to tell — the story of Pancho Pillow — it'll wipe you out, man. No bullshit. Let's have lunch, Fletch. Just you and Marge and me and Beatriz and Idaho. We'll have a picnic. We'll go up to the volcano."

The lights went out. There was silence for a fraction of a second, and in that splinter of time Fletch had covered the distance between Pancho and the open doorway. He was not quite in the street when the chorus of groans broke. La Beatriz screamed.

"Adiós, you fuckin' monsters," Fletch shouted indignantly.

"Fletch!" Pancho Pillow cried. "For Christ's sake!" His voice was sheer desperation.

Monsters, Fletch thought. Flying men. The street down which he ran was packed with drunken invisible soldiers. Men walked about striking matches and falling down in the road. The military police approached with their flashlights; Fletch huddled in the doorway of the cinema to let them pass. As he ran across the square, they turned their lights on him and shouted.

Fletch laughed. Never in his life had he so appreciated modern technology. Fine, he thought, bring the jungle to the folks.

At the market café, they had lighted hurricane lamps. A few trucks were parked outside, and the first in line was an International Harvester pickup truck loaded with chickens. A man in a Stetson was inspecting the carburetor. He was very drunk and singing to himself.

Fletch approached and asked him, with elaborate courtesy, for a ride to the coast. The man turned to him and crooned the refrain of his song, to illustrate the futility of all ambition. Fletch offered to hold his flashlight and offered twice the reasonable price for a ride, so when the truck started through the dark streets he was safely aboard. As they passed the square, Fletch could see Pancho Pillow's Lincoln cruising like a baffled predator.

"Fuck 'em all," Fletch told the driver.

"Fuck," the driver agreed. He was so drunk it seemed impossible to think of him driving down the mountains. A little girl in braids was nestled in the space behind the seat, asleep. When the wind and the noise of the engine permitted, Fletch could hear the chickens in the back of the truck.

The man in the Stetson drove much too fast and his clutch

seemed to be slipping badly. Halfway down to the coast, as they
sped past banana trees, he began to sing again.

"You warned me over and over," he sang,

> You kept warning me about the woman
> That she wasn't a good woman for me
> You gave me so many warnings
> So many warnings
> That I thought you had gone loco
> But the warning you should have given me
> Was the one you didn't give me
> That you were a thieving betrayer
> Just as bad as her
> So now it's me that's gone loco
> And I got a warning for you!

At times, Fletch sang with him. It was still dark when they
reached the coast road, but the moon was very bright and Fletch
could see the breakers beyond the beach.

He got out, paid the driver and walked along the beach toward his house, guided by the dark mass of the bay headlands.
He was still walking when the sun came up over the volcano
and woke the birds and lit the sea to pink and pale green beyond
imagining. Now and then he passed men sleeping on the sand.

His house, when he came to it, was silent, although he could
hear Doña Laura awake next door. Willie Wings was sprawled
on the hammock before the doorway, quite awake and watching him blankly. The parrot lay prone and stiff in its cage, covered with a second skin of white dust. The morning flies had
started to gather on it.

Fletch went past Willie Wings and inside. His children were
asleep on their cot in the kitchen, but he heard faint voices from
the bedroom. He got down on his hands and knees and crept
silently over the tiles toward the bamboo curtain that divided
the house.

Lifting the curtain slightly, he saw Marge and Fencer together on the mattress, naked. Marge's long tanned body entwined Fencer's like a constricting serpent. Fencer was clutching her around the thighs as though he were afraid she would fall. Their faces were together.

"I wish he hadn't bolted," Fencer was saying.

It occurred to Fletch that he could not be certain that Fencer had not heard him come in.

"You know, like he just bolted. It looked for a while like we were really going to get something going together. I thought, by God, it's gonna work, we'll go up there and turn on and we'll groove and we'll break down the verbal barrier. But he bolted."

"Well, my God," Marge said, "it was pretty stupid of Willie Wings to shoot at him. For Christ's sake, he's so paranoid *anyway.*"

"Willie's a fanatic," Fencer said. He ran his hands over Marge's backside. "I'm kind of a fanatic too."

She took his long hair in her hands and pulled it round his neck and kissed him.

"You super-romantic shithead," she said.

Fletch lay still on the tiles trying to hold his breath and watched them do it. When his ribs began to hurt, he turned over and slid across the cool floor to the doorway. It took him nearly five minutes to crawl out — a masterpiece of silence.

When he was outside, he picked up one of the weights he had bought to keep himself in condition and lay down with it. Lying on his back, he held the weight at arm's length for quite a long time. Sweat welled from his body. Then he lowered the weight and looked at the sky.

"Willie Wings," he said to Willie Wings, "I went up that mountain, right? You were there, you saw me do it, right?"

"Yeah," Willie said. "Not all the way. But you went up the mountain."

"Right," Fletch said. "I went up." He leaned his head back to look at Willie. "I went up. And you should have been there to see me come *down,* man. Because *that* was really something else."

Willie Wings watched him for a little while.

"Fletch, babe," he said. "I had you wrong, brother. You really are a poet."

HELPING

➤

ONE GRAY November day, Elliot went to Boston for the afternoon. The wet streets seemed cold and lonely. He sensed a broken promise in the city's elegance and verve. Old hopes tormented him like phantom limbs, but he did not drink. He had joined Alcoholics Anonymous fifteen months before.

Christmas came, childless, a festival of regret. His wife went to Mass and cooked a turkey. Sober, Elliot walked in the woods.

In January, blizzards swept down from the Arctic until the weather became too cold for snow. The Shawmut Valley grew quiet and crystalline. In the white silences, Elliot could hear the boards of his house contract and feel a shrinking in his bones. Each dusk, starveling deer came out of the wooded swamp behind the house to graze his orchard for whatever raccoons had uncovered and left behind. At night he lay beside his sleeping wife listening to the baying of dog packs running them down in the deep moon-shadowed snow.

Day in, day out, he was sober. At times it was almost stimulating. But he could not shake off the sensations he had felt in Boston. In his mind's eye he could see dead leaves rattling along brick gutters and savor that day's desperation. The brief outing had undermined him.

Sober, however, he remained, until the day a man named

Blankenship came into his office at the state hospital for counseling. Blankenship had red hair, a brutal face and a sneaking
manner. He was a sponger and petty thief whom Elliot had seen
a number of times before.

"I been having this dream," Blankenship announced loudly.
His voice was not pleasant. His skin was unwholesome. Every
time he got arrested the court sent him to the psychiatrists and
the psychiatrists, who spoke little English, sent him to Elliot.

Blankenship had joined the army after his first burglary but
had never served east of the Rhine. After a few months in Wies-
baden, he had been discharged for reasons of unsuitability, but
he told everyone he was a veteran of the Vietnam War. He went
about in a tiger suit. Elliot had had enough of him.

"Dreams are boring," Elliot told him.

Blankenship was outraged. "Whaddaya mean?" he demanded.

During counseling sessions Elliot usually moved his chair into
the middle of the room in order to seem accessible to his cli-
ents. Now he stayed securely behind his desk. He did not care to
seem accessible to Blankenship. "What I said, Mr. Blankenship.
Other people's dreams are boring. Didn't you ever hear that?"

"Boring?" Blankenship frowned. He seemed unable to imagine a meaning for the word.

Elliot picked up a pencil and set its point quivering on his
desktop blotter. He gazed into his client's slack-jawed face. The
Blankenship family made their way through life as strolling
litigants, and young Blankenship's specialty was slipping on ice
cubes. Hauled off the pavement, he would hassle the doctors in
Emergency for pain pills and hurry to a law clinic. The Blanken-
ships had threatened suit against half the property owners in the
southern part of the state. What they could not extort at law
they stole. But even the Blankenship family had abandoned
Blankenship. His last visit to the hospital had been subsequent

to an arrest for lifting a case of hot-dog rolls from Woolworth's. He lived in a Goodwill depository bin in Wyndham.

"Now I suppose you want to tell me your dream. Is that right, Mr. Blankenship?"

Blankenship looked left and right like a dog surrendering eye contact. "Don't you want to hear it?" he asked humbly.

Elliot was unmoved. "Tell me something, Blankenship. Was your dream about Vietnam?"

At the mention of the word "Vietnam," Blankenship customarily broke into a broad smile. Now he looked guilty and guarded. He shrugged. "Ya."

"How come you have dreams about that place, Blankenship? You were never there."

"Whaddaya mean?" Blankenship began to say, but Elliot cut him off.

"You were never there, my man. You never saw the goddamn place. You have no business dreaming about it! You better cut it out!"

He had raised his voice to the extent that the secretary outside his open door paused at her computer.

"Lemme alone," Blankenship said fearfully. "Some doctor you are."

"It's all right," Elliot assured him. "I'm not a doctor."

"Everybody's on my case," Blankenship said. His moods were volatile. He began to weep.

Elliot watched the tears roll down Blankenship's chapped, pitted cheeks. He cleared his throat. "Look, fella . . ." he began. He felt at a loss. He felt like telling Blankenship that things were tough all over.

Blankenship sniffed and telescoped his neck and after a moment looked at Elliot. His look was disconcertingly trustful; he was used to being counseled.

"Really, you know, it's ridiculous for you to tell me your

problems have to do with Nam. You were never over there. It was me over there, Blankenship. Not you."

Blankenship leaned forward and put his forehead on his knees.

"Your troubles have to do with here and now," Elliot told his client. "Fantasies aren't helpful."

His voice sounded overripe and hypocritical in his own ears. What a dreadful business, he thought. What an awful job this is. Anger was driving him crazy.

Blankenship straightened up and spoke through his tears. "This dream . . ." he said. "I'm scared."

Elliot felt ready to endure a great deal in order not to hear Blankenship's dream.

"I'm not the one you see about that," he said. In the end he knew his duty. He sighed. "OK. All right. Tell me about it."

"Yeah?" Blankenship asked with leaden sarcasm. "Yeah? You think dreams are friggin' boring!"

"No, no," Elliot said. He offered Blankenship a tissue and Blankenship took one. "That was sort of off the top of my head. I didn't really mean it."

Blankenship fixed his eyes on dreaming distance. "There's a feeling that goes with it. With the dream." Then he shook his head in revulsion and looked at Elliot as though he had only just awakened. "So what do you think? You think it's boring?"

"Of course not," Elliot said. "A physical feeling?"

"Ya. It's like I'm floating in rubber."

He watched Elliot stealthily, aware of quickened attention. Elliot had caught dengue in Vietnam and during his weeks of delirium had felt vaguely as though he were floating in rubber.

"What are you seeing in this dream?"

Blankenship only shook his head. Elliot suffered a brief but intense attack of rage.

"Hey, Blankenship," he said equably, "here I am, man. You can see I'm listening."

"What I saw was black," Blankenship said. He spoke in an odd tremolo. His behavior was quite different from anything Elliot had come to expect from him.

"Black? What was it?"

"Smoke. The sky maybe."

"The sky?" Elliot asked.

"It was all black. I was scared."

In a waking dream of his own, Elliot felt the muscles on his neck distend. He was looking up at a sky that was black, filled with smoke-swollen clouds, lit with fires, damped with blood and rain.

"What were you scared of?" he asked Blankenship.

"I don't know," Blankenship said.

Elliot could not drive the black sky from his inward eye. It was as though Blankenship's dream had infected his own mind.

"You don't know? You don't know what you were scared of?"

Blankenship's posture was rigid. Elliot, who knew the aspect of true fear, recognized it there in front of him.

"The Nam," Blankenship said.

"You're not even old enough," Elliot told him.

Blankenship sat trembling with joined palms between his thighs. His face was flushed and not in the least ennobled by pain. He had trouble with alcohol and drugs. He had trouble with everything.

"So wherever your black sky is, it isn't Vietnam."

Things were so unfair, Elliot thought. It was unfair of Blankenship to appropriate the condition of a Vietnam veteran. The trauma inducing his post-traumatic stress had been nothing more serious than his own birth, a routine procedure. Now, in addition to the poverty, anxiety and confusion that would always be his life's lot, he had been visited with irony. It was all arbitrary and some people simply got elected. Everyone knew that who had been where Blankenship had not.

"Because, I assure you, Mr. Blankenship, you were never there."

"Whaddaya mean?" Blankenship asked.

When Blankenship was gone, Elliot leafed through his file and saw that the psychiatrists had passed him upstairs without recording a diagnosis. Disproportionately angry, he went out to the secretary's desk.

"Nobody wrote up that last patient," he said. "I'm not supposed to see people without a diagnosis. The shrinks are just passing the buck."

The secretary was a tall, solemn redhead with prominent front teeth and a slight speech disorder. "Dr. Sayyid will have kittens if he hears you call him a shrink, Chas. He's already complained. He hates being called a shrink."

"Then he came to the wrong country," Elliot said. "He can go back to his own."

The woman giggled. "He *is* the doctor, Chas."

"Hates being called a shrink!" He threw the file on the secretary's table and stormed back toward his office. "That fucking little zip couldn't give you a decent haircut. He's a prescription clerk."

The secretary looked about her guiltily and shook her head. She was used to him.

Elliot succeeded in calming himself down after a while, but the image of black sky remained with him. At first he thought he would be able to shrug the whole thing off. After a few minutes, he picked up his phone and dialed Blankenship's probation officer.

"The Vietnam thing is all he has," the probation officer explained. "I guess he picked it up around."

"His descriptions are vivid," Elliot said.

"You mean they sound authentic?"

"I mean he had me going today. He was ringing my bells."

"Good for Blanky. Think he believes it himself?"

"Yes," Elliot said. "He believes it himself now."

Elliot told the probation officer about Blankenship's current arrest, which was for showering illegally at midnight in the Wyndham Regional High School. He asked what Probation knew about Blankenship's present relationship with his family.

"You kiddin'?" the P.O. asked. "They're all locked down. The whole family's inside. The old man's in Bridgewater. Little Donny's in San Quentin or somewhere. Their dog's in the pound."

Elliot had lunch alone in the hospital staff cafeteria. On the far side of the double-glazed windows, the day was darkening as an expected snowstorm gathered. Along Route 7, ancient elms stood frozen against the gray sky. When he had finished his sandwich and coffee, he sat staring out at the winter afternoon. His anger had given way to an insistent anxiety.

On the way back to his office, he stopped at the hospital gift shop for a copy of *Sports Illustrated* and a candy bar. When he was inside again, he closed the door and put his feet up. It was Friday and he had no appointments for the remainder of the day, nothing to do but write a few letters and read the office mail.

Elliot's cubicle in the social services department was windowless and lined with bookshelves. When he found himself unable to concentrate on the magazine and without any heart for his paperwork, he ran his eye over the row of books beside his chair. There were volumes by Heinrich Muller and Carlos Castaneda, Jones's life of Freud and *The Golden Bough*. The books aroused a revulsion in Elliot. Their present uselessness repelled him.

Over and over again, detail by detail, he tried to recall his conversation with Blankenship.

"You were never there," he heard himself explaining. He was

trying to get the whole incident straightened out after the fact. Something was wrong. Dread crept over him like a paralysis. He ate his candy bar without tasting it. He knew that the craving for sweets was itself a bad sign.

Blankenship had misappropriated someone else's dream and made it his own. It made no difference whether you had been there, after all. The dreams had crossed the ocean. They were in the air.

He took his glasses off and put them on his desk and sat with his arms folded, looking into the well of light from his desk lamp. There seemed to be nothing but whirl inside him. Unwelcome things came and went in his mind's eye. His heart beat faster. He could not control the headlong promiscuity of his thoughts.

It was possible to imagine larval dreams traveling in suspended animation undetectable in a host brain. They could be divided and regenerate like flatworms, hide in seams and bedding, in war stories, laughter, snapshots. They could rot your socks and turn your memory into a black and green blister. Green for the hills, black for the sky above. At daybreak they hung themselves up in rows like bats. At dusk they went out to look for dreamers.

Elliot put his jacket on and went into the outer office, where the secretary sat frowning into the measured sound and light of her machine. She must enjoy its sleekness and order, he thought. She was divorced. Four red-headed kids between ten and seventeen lived with her in an unpainted house across from Stop & Shop. Elliot liked her and had come to find her attractive. He managed a smile for her.

"Ethel, I think I'm going to pack it in," he declared. It seemed awkward to be leaving early without a reason.

"Jack wants to talk to you before you go, Chas."

Elliot looked at her blankly.

Then his colleague, Jack Sprague, having heard his voice,

called from the adjoining cubicle. "Chas, what about Sunday's games? Shall I call you with the spread?"

"I don't know," Elliot said. "I'll phone you tomorrow."

"This is a big decision for him," Jack Sprague told the secretary. "He might lose twenty-five bucks."

At present, Elliot drew a slightly higher salary than Jack Sprague, although Jack had a Ph.D. and Elliot was only an M.S.W. Different branches of the state government employed them.

"Twenty-five bucks," said the woman. "If you guys have no better use for twenty-five bucks, give it to me."

"Where are you off to, by the way?" Sprague asked.

Elliot began to answer, but for a moment no reply occurred to him. He shrugged. "I have to get back," he finally stammered. "I promised Grace."

"Was that Blankenship I saw leaving?"

Elliot nodded.

"It's February," Jack said. "How come he's not in Florida?"

"I don't know," Elliot said. He put on his coat and walked to the door. "I'll see you."

"Have a nice weekend," the secretary said. She and Sprague looked after him indulgently as he walked toward the main corridor.

"Are Chas and Grace going out on the town?" she said to Sprague. "What do you think?"

"That would be the day," Sprague said. "Tomorrow he'll come back over here and read all day. He spends every weekend holed up in this goddamn office while she does something or other at the church." He shook his head. "Every night he's at A.A. and she's home alone."

Ethel savored her overbite. "Jack," she said teasingly, "are you thinking what I think you're thinking? Shame on you."

"I'm thinking I'm glad I'm not him, that's what I'm thinking. That's as much as I'll say."

"Yeah, well, I don't care," Ethel said. "Two salaries and no kids, that's the way to go, boy."

Elliot went out through the automatic doors of the emergency bay and the cold closed over him. He walked across the hospital parking lot with his eyes on the pavement, his hands thrust deep in his overcoat pockets, skirting patches of shattered ice. There was no wind, but the motionless air stung; the metal frames of his glasses burned his skin. Curlicues of mud-brown ice coated the soiled snowbanks along the street. Although it was still afternoon, the street lights had come on.

The lock on his car door had frozen and he had to breathe on the keyhole to fit the key. When the engine turned over, Jussi Björling's recording of the Handel Largo filled the car interior. He snapped it off at once.

Halted at the first stoplight, he began to feel the want of a destination. The fear and impulse to flight that had got him out of the office faded, and he had no desire to go home. He was troubled by a peculiar impatience that might have been with time itself. It was as though he were waiting for something. The sensation made him feel anxious; it was unfamiliar but not altogether unpleasant. When the light changed he drove on, past the Gulf station and the firehouse and between the greens of Ilford Common. At the far end of the common he swung into the parking lot of the Packard Conway Library and stopped with the engine running. What he was experiencing, he thought, was the principle of possibility.

He turned off the engine and went out again into the cold. Behind the leaded library windows he could see the librarian pouring coffee in her tiny private office. The librarian was a Quaker of socialist convictions named Candace Music, who was Elliot's cousin.

The Conway Library was all dark wood and etched mirrors,

a Gothic saloon. Years before, out of work and booze-whipped, Elliot had gone to hide there. Because Candace was a classicist's widow and knew some Greek, she was one of the few people in the valley with whom Elliot had cared to speak in those days. Eventually, it had seemed to him that all their conversations tended toward Vietnam, so he had gone less and less often. Elliot was the only Vietnam veteran Candace knew well enough to chat with, and he had come to suspect that he was being probed for the edification of the East Ilford Friends Meeting. At that time he had still pretended to talk easily about his war and had prepared little discourses and picaresque anecdotes to recite on demand. Earnest seekers like Candace had caused him great secret distress.

Candace came out of her office to find him at the checkout desk. He watched her brow furrow with concern as she composed a smile. "Chas, what a surprise. You haven't been in for an age."

"Sure I have, Candace. I went to all the Wednesday films last fall. I work just across the road."

"I know, dear," Candace said. "I always seem to miss you."

A cozy fire burned in the hearth, an antique brass clock ticked along on the marble mantel above it. On a couch near the fireplace an old man sat upright, his mouth open, asleep among half a dozen soiled plastic bags. Two teenage girls whispered over their homework at a table under the largest window.

"Now that I'm here," he said, laughing, "I can't remember what I came to get."

"Stay and get warm," Candace told him. "Got a minute? Have a cup of coffee."

Elliot had nothing but time, but he quickly realized that he did not want to stay and pass it with Candace. He had no clear idea of why he had come to the library. Standing at the checkout desk, he accepted coffee. She attended him with an air of benign supervision, as though he were a Chinese peasant and she a medical missionary, like her father. Candace was tall and plain, more handsome in her middle sixties than she had ever been.

"Why don't we sit down?"

He allowed her to gentle him into a chair by the fire. They made a threesome with the sleeping old man.

"Have you given up translating, Chas? I hope not."

"Not at all," he said. Together they had once rendered a few fragments of Sophocles into verse. She was good at clever rhymes.

"You come in so rarely, Chas. Ted's books go to waste."

After her husband's death, Candace had donated his books to the Conway, where they reposed in a reading room inscribed to his memory, untouched among foreign-language volumes, local genealogies and books in large type for the elderly.

"I have a study in the barn," he told Candace. "I work there. When I have time." The lie was absurd, but he felt the need of it.

"And you're working with Vietnam veterans," Candace declared.

"Supposedly," Elliot said. He was growing impatient with her nodding solicitude.

"Actually," he said, "I came in for the new Oxford *Classical World*. I thought you'd get it for the library and I could have a look before I spent my hard-earned cash."

Candace beamed. "You've come to the right place, Chas, I'm happy to say." He thought she looked disproportionately happy. "I have it."

"Good," Elliot said, standing. "I'll just take it, then. I can't really stay."

Candace took his cup and saucer and stood as he did. When the library telephone rang, she ignored it, reluctant to let him go. "How's Grace?" she asked.

"Fine," Elliot said. "Grace is well."

At the third ring she went to the desk. When her back was turned, he hesitated for a moment and then went outside.

The gray afternoon had softened into night, and it was snowing. The falling snow whirled like a furious mist in the headlight beams on Route 7 and settled implacably on Elliot's cheeks and eyelids. His heart, for no good reason, leaped up in childlike expectation. He had run away from a dream and encountered possibility. He felt in possession of a promise. He began to walk toward the roadside lights.

Only gradually did he begin to understand what had brought him there and what the happy anticipation was that fluttered in his breast. Drinking, he had started his evenings from the Conway Library. He would arrive hung over in the early afternoon to browse and read. When the old pain rolled in with dusk, he would walk down to the Midway Tavern for a remedy. Standing in the snow outside the library, he realized that he had contrived to promise himself a drink.

Ahead, through the storm, he could see the beer signs in the Midway's window warm and welcoming. Snowflakes spun around his head like an excitement.

Outside the Midway's package store, he paused with his hand on the doorknob. There was an old man behind the counter whom Elliot remembered from his drinking days. When he was inside, he realized that the old man neither knew nor cared who he was. The package store was thick with dust; it was on the counter, the shelves, the bottles themselves. The old counterman looked dusty. Elliot bought a bottle of King William Scotch and put it in the inside pocket of his overcoat.

Passing the windows of the Midway Tavern, Elliot could see the ranks of bottles aglow behind the bar. The place was crowded with men leaving the afternoon shifts at the shoe and felt factories. No one turned to note him when he passed inside. There was a single stool vacant at the bar and he took it. His heart beat faster. Bruce Springsteen was on the jukebox.

The bartender was a club fighter from Pittsfield called Jackie G., with whom Elliot had often gossiped. Jackie G. greeted him as though he had been in the previous evening. "Say, babe?"

"How do," Elliot said.

A couple of the men at the bar eyed his shirt and tie. Confronted with the bartender, he felt impelled to explain his presence. "Just thought I'd stop by," he told Jackie G. "Just thought I'd have one. Saw the light. The snow . . ." He chuckled expansively.

"Good move," the bartender said. "Scotch?"

"Double," Elliot said.

When he shoved two dollars forward along the bar, Jackie G. pushed one of the bills back to him. "Happy hour, babe."

"Ah," Elliot said. He watched Jackie pour the double. "Not a moment too soon."

For five minutes or so, Elliot sat in his car in the barn with the engine running and his Handel tape on full volume. He had driven over from East Ilford in a Baroque ecstasy, swinging and swaying and singing along. When the tape ended, he turned off the engine and poured some Scotch into an apple juice container to store providentially beneath the car seat. Then he took the tape and the Scotch into the house with him. He was lying on the sofa in the dark living room, listening to the Largo, when he heard his wife's car in the driveway. By the time Grace had made her way up the icy back-porch steps, he was able to hide the Scotch and rinse his glass clean in the kitchen sink. The drinking life, he thought, was lived moment by moment.

Soon she was in the tiny cloakroom struggling off with her overcoat. In the process she knocked over a cross-country ski, which stood propped against the cloakroom wall. It had been more than a year since Elliot had used the skis.

She came into the kitchen and sat down at the table to take off her boots. Her lean, freckled face was flushed with the cold, but her eyes looked weary. "I wish you'd put those skis down in the barn," she told him. "You never use them."

"I always like to think," Elliot said, "that I'll start the morning off skiing."

"Well, you never do," she said. "How long have you been home?"

"Practically just walked in," he said. Her pointing out that he no longer skied in the morning enraged him. "I stopped at the Conway Library to get the new Oxford *Classical World*. Candace ordered it."

Her look grew troubled. She had caught something in his voice. With dread and bitter satisfaction, Elliot watched his wife detect the smell of whiskey.

"Oh God," she said. "I don't believe it."

Let's get it over with, he thought. Let's have the song and dance.

She sat up straight in her chair and looked at him in fear.

"Oh, Chas," she said, "how could you?"

For a moment he was tempted to try to explain it all.

"The fact is," Elliot told his wife, "I hate people who start the day cross-country skiing."

She shook her head in denial and leaned her forehead on her palm and cried.

He looked into the kitchen window and saw his own distorted image. "The fact is I think I'll start tomorrow morning by stringing head-high razor wire across Anderson's trail."

The Andersons were the Elliots' nearest neighbors. Loyall Anderson was a full professor of government at the state university, thirty miles away. Anderson and his wife were blond and both of them were over six feet tall. They had two blond children, who qualified for the gifted class in the local school but attended regular classes in token of the Andersons' opposition to elitism.

"Sure," Elliot said. "Stringing wire's good exercise. It's life-affirming in its own way."

The Andersons started each and every day with a brisk morning glide along a trail that they partly maintained. They skied well and presented a pleasing, wholesome sight. If, in the course of their adventure, they encountered a snowmobile, Darlene Anderson would affect to choke and cough, indicating her displeasure. If the snowmobile approached them from behind and the trail was narrow, the Andersons would decline to let it pass, asserting their statutory right-of-way.

"I don't want to hear your violent fantasies," Grace said.

Elliot was picturing razor wire, the army kind. He was picturing the decapitated Andersons, their blood and jaunty ski caps bright on the white trail. He was picturing their severed heads, their earnest blue eyes and large white teeth reflecting the virginal morning snow. Although Elliot hated snowmobiles, he hated the Andersons far more.

He looked at his wife and saw that she had stopped crying. Her long, elegant face was rigid and lipless.

"Know what I mean? One string at mommy-and-daddy level for Loyall and Darlene. And a bitty wee string at kiddie level for Skippy and Samantha, those cunning little whizzes."

"Stop it," she said to him.

"Sorry," Elliot told her.

Stiff with shame, he went and took his bottle out of the cabinet into which he had thrust it and poured a drink. He was aware of her eyes on him. As he drank, a fragment from old Music's translation of *Medea* came into his mind. "Old friend, I have to weep. The gods and I went mad together and made things as they are." It was such a waste; eighteen months of struggle thrown away. But there was no way to get the stuff back in the bottle.

"I'm very sorry," he said. "You know I'm very sorry, don't you, Grace?"

The delectable Handel arias spun on in the next room.

"You must stop," she said. "You must make yourself stop before it takes over."

"It's out of my hands," Elliot said. He showed her his empty hands. "It's beyond me."

"You'll lose your job, Chas." She stood up at the table and leaned on it, staring wide-eyed at him. Drunk as he was, the panic in her voice frightened him. "You'll end up in jail again."

"One engages," Elliot said, "and then one sees."

"How can you have done it?" she demanded. "You promised me."

"First the promises," Elliot said, "and then the rest.",

"Last time was supposed to be the last time," she said.

"Yes," he said, "I remember."

"I can't stand it," she said. "You reduce me to hysterics." She wrung her hands for him to see. "See? Here I am, I'm in hysterics."

"What can I say?" Elliot asked. He went to the bottle and refilled his glass. "Maybe you shouldn't watch."

"You want me to be forbearing, Chas? I'm not going to be."

"The last thing I want," Elliot said, "is an argument."

"I'll give you a fucking argument. You didn't have to drink. All you had to do was come home."

"That must have been the problem," he said.

Then he ducked, alert at the last possible second to the missile that came for him at hairline level. Covering up, he heard the shattering of glass, and a fine rain of crystals enveloped him. She had sailed the sugar bowl at him; it had smashed against the wall above his head and there was sugar and glass in his hair.

"You bastard!" she screamed. "You are undermining me!"

"You ought not to throw things at me," Elliot said. "I don't throw things at you."

He left her frozen into her follow-through and went into the living room to turn the music off. When he returned she was leaning back against the wall, rubbing her right elbow with her left hand. Her eyes were bright. She had picked up one of her boots from the middle of the kitchen floor and stood holding it.

"What the hell do you mean, that must have been the problem?"

He set his glass on the edge of the sink with an unsteady hand and turned to her. "What do I mean? I mean that most of the time I'm putting one foot in front of the other like a good soldier and I'm out of it from the neck up. But there are times when I don't think I will ever be dead enough — or dead long enough — to get the taste of this life off my teeth. That's what I mean!"

She looked at him dry-eyed. "Poor fella," she said.

"What you have to understand, Grace, is that this drink I'm having" — he raised the glass toward her in a gesture of salute — "is the only worthwhile thing I've done in the last year and a half. It's the only thing in my life that means jack shit, the closest thing to satisfaction I've had. Now how can you begrudge me that? It's the best I'm capable of."

"You'll go too far," she said to him. "You'll see."

"What's that, Grace? A threat to walk?" He was grinding his teeth. "Don't make me laugh. You, walk? You, the friend of the unfortunate?"

"Don't you hit me," she said when she looked at his face. "Don't you dare."

"You, the Christian Queen of Calvary, walk? Why, I don't believe that for a minute."

She ran a hand through her hair and bit her lip. "No, we stay," she said. Anger and distraction made her look young. Her cheeks blazed rosy against the general pallor of her skin. "In my family we stay until the fella dies. That's the tradition. We stay and pour it for them and they die."

He put his drink down and shook his head.

"I thought we'd come through," Grace said. "I was sure."

"No," Elliot said. "Not altogether."

They stood in silence for a minute. Elliot sat down at the oilcloth-covered table. Grace walked around it and poured herself a whiskey.

"You are undermining me, Chas. You are making things impossible for me and I just don't know." She drank and winced. "I'm not going to stay through another drunk. I'm telling you right now. I haven't got it in me. I'll die."

He did not want to look at her. He watched the flakes settle against the glass of the kitchen door. "Do what you feel the need of," he said.

"I just can't take it," she said. Her voice was not scolding but measured and reasonable. "It's February. And I went to court this morning and lost Vopotik."

Once again, he thought, my troubles are going to be obviated by those of the deserving poor. He said, "Which one was that?"

"Don't you remember them? The three-year-old with the broken fingers?"

He shrugged. Grace sipped her whiskey.

"I told you. I said I had a three-year-old with broken fingers, and you said, 'Maybe he owed somebody money.'"

"Yes," he said, "I remember now."

"You ought to see the Vopotiks, Chas. The woman is young and obese. She's so young that for a while I thought I could get to her as a juvenile. The guy is a biker. They believe the kid came from another planet to control their lives. They believe this literally, both of them."

"You shouldn't get involved that way," Elliot said. "You should leave it to the caseworkers."

"They scared their first caseworker all the way to California. They were following me to work."

"You didn't tell me."

"Are you kidding?" she asked. "Of course I didn't." To Elliot's surprise, his wife poured herself a second whiskey. "You know how they address the child? As 'dude.' She says to it, 'Hey, dude.'" Grace shuddered with loathing. "You can't imagine! The woman munching Twinkies. The kid smelling of shit. They're high morning, noon and night, but you can't get anybody for that these days."

"People must really hate it," Elliot said, "when somebody tells them they're not treating their kids right."

"They definitely don't want to hear it," Grace said. "You're right." She sat stirring her drink, frowning into the glass. "The Vopotik child will die, I think."

"Surely not," Elliot said.

"This one I think will die," Grace said. She took a deep breath and puffed out her cheeks and looked at him forlornly. "The situation's extreme. Of course, sometimes you wonder whether it makes any difference. That's the big question, isn't it?"

"I would think," Elliot said, "that would be the one question you didn't ask."

"But you do," she said. "You wonder: Ought they to live at all? To continue the cycle?" She put a hand to her hair and shook her head as if in confusion. "Some of these folks, my God, the poor things cannot put Wednesday on top of Tuesday to save their lives."

"It's a trick," Elliot agreed, "a lot of them can't manage."

"And kids are small, they're handy and underfoot. They make noise. They can't hurt you back."

"I suppose child abuse is something people can do together," Elliot said.

"Some kids are obnoxious. No question about it."

"I wouldn't know," Elliot said.

"Maybe you should stop complaining. Maybe you're better off. Maybe your kids are better off unborn."

"Better off or not," Elliot said, "it looks like they'll stay that way."

"I mean our kids, of course," Grace said. "I'm not blaming you, understand? It's just that here we are with you drunk again and me losing Vopotik, so I thought why not get into the big unaskable questions." She got up and folded her arms and began to pace up and down the kitchen. "Oh," she said when her eye fell upon the bottle, "that's good stuff, Chas. You won't mind if I have another? I'll leave you enough to get loaded on."

Elliot watched her pour. So much pain, he thought; such anger and confusion. He was tired of pain, anger and confusion; they were what had got him in trouble that very morning.

The liquor seemed to be giving him a perverse lucidity when all he now required was oblivion. His rage, especially, was intact in its salting of alcohol. Its contours were palpable and bleeding at the borders. Booze was good for rage. Booze could keep it burning through the darkest night.

"What happened in court?" he asked his wife.

She was leaning on one arm against the wall, her long, strong body flexed at the hip. Holding her glass, she stared angrily toward the invisible fields outside. "I lost the child," she said.

Elliot thought that a peculiar way of putting it. He said nothing.

"The court convened in an atmosphere of high hilarity. It may be Hate Month around here but it was buddy-buddy over at Ilford Courthouse. The room was full of bikers and bikers' lawyers. A colorful crowd. There was a lot of bonding." She drank and shivered. "They didn't think too well of me. They don't think too well of broads as lawyers. Neither does the judge. The judge has the common touch. He's one of the boys."

"Which judge?" Elliot asked.

"Buckley. A man of about sixty. Know him? Lots of veins on his nose?"

Elliot shrugged.

"I thought I had done my homework," Grace told him. "But suddenly I had nothing but paper. No witnesses. It was Margolis at Valley Hospital who spotted the radiator burns. He called us in the first place. Suddenly he's got to keep his reservation for a campsite in St. John. So Buckley threw his deposition out." She began to chew on a fingernail. "The caseworkers have vanished — one's in L.A., the other's in Nepal. I went in there and got run over. I lost the child."

"It happens all the time," Elliot said. "Doesn't it?"

"This one shouldn't have been lost, Chas. These people aren't simply confused. They're weird. They stink."

"You go messing into anybody's life," Elliot said, "that's what you'll find."

"If the child stays in that house," she said, "he's going to die."

"You did your best," he told his wife. "Forget it."

She pushed the bottle away. She was holding a water glass that was almost a third full of whiskey.

"That's what the commissioner said."

Elliot was thinking of how she must have looked in court to the cherry-faced judge and the bikers and their lawyers. Like the schoolteachers who had tormented their childhoods, earnest and tight-assed, humorless and self-righteous. It was not surprising that things had gone against her.

He walked over to the window and faced his reflection again. "Your optimism always surprises me."

"My optimism? Where I grew up our principal cultural expression was the funeral. Whatever keeps me going, it isn't optimism."

"No?" he asked. "What is it?"

"I forget," she said.

"Maybe it's your religious perspective. Your sense of the divine plan."

She sighed in exasperation. "Look, I don't think I want to fight anymore. I'm sorry I threw the sugar at you. I'm not your keeper. Pick on someone your own size."

"Sometimes," Elliot said, "I try to imagine what it's like to believe that the sky is full of care and concern."

"You want to take everything from me, do you?" She stood leaning against the back of her chair. "That you can't take. It's the only part of my life you can't mess up."

He was thinking that if it had not been for her he might not have survived. There could be no forgiveness for that. "Your life? You've got all this piety strung out between Monadnock and Central America. And look at yourself. Look at your life."

"Yes," she said, "look at it."

"You should have been a nun. You don't know how to live."

"I know that," she said. "That's why I stopped doing counseling. Because I'd rather talk the law than life." She turned to him. "You got everything I had, Chas. What's left I absolutely require."

"I swear I would rather be a drunk," Elliot said, "than force myself to believe such trivial horseshit."

"Well, you're going to have to do it without a straight man," she said, "because this time I'm not going to be here for you. Believe it or not."

"I don't believe it," Elliot said. "Not my Grace."

"You're really good at this," she told him. "You make me feel ashamed of my own name."

"I love your name," he said.

The telephone rang. They let it ring three times, and then Elliot went over and answered it.

"Hey, who's that?" a good-humored voice on the phone demanded.

Elliot recited their phone number.

"Hey, I want to talk to your woman, man. Put her on."

"I'll give her a message," Elliot said.

"You put your woman on, man. Run and get her."

Elliot looked at the receiver. He shook his head. "Mr. Vopotik?"

"Never you fuckin' mind, man. I don't want to talk to you. I want to talk to the skinny bitch."

Elliot hung up.

"Is it him?" she asked.

"I guess so."

They waited for the phone to ring again and it shortly did.

"I'll talk to him," Grace said. But Elliot already had the phone.

"Who are you, asshole?" the voice inquired. "What's your fuckin' name, man?"

"Elliot," Elliot said.

"Hey, don't hang up on me, Elliot. I won't put up with that. I told you go get that skinny bitch, man. You go do it."

There were sounds of festivity in the background on the other end of the line — a stereo and drunken voices.

"Hey," the voice declared. "Hey, don't keep me waiting, man."

"What do you want to say to her?" Elliot asked.

"That's none of your fucking business, fool. Do what I told you."

"My wife is resting," Elliot said. "I'm taking her calls."

He was answered by a shout of rage. He put the phone aside for a moment and finished his glass of whiskey. When he picked it up again the man on the line was screaming at him. "That bitch tried to break up my family, man! She almost got away with it. You know what kind of pain my wife went through?"

"What kind?" Elliot asked.

For a few seconds he heard only the noise of the party. "Hey, you're not drunk, are you, fella?"

"Certainly not," Elliot insisted.

"You tell that skinny bitch she's gonna pay for what she did to my family, man. You tell her she can run but she can't hide. I don't care where you go — California, anywhere — I'll get to you."

"Now that I have you on the phone," Elliot said, "I'd like to ask you a couple of questions. Promise you won't get mad?"

"Stop it!" Grace said to him. She tried to wrench the phone from his grasp, but he clutched it to his chest.

"Do you keep a journal?" Elliot asked the man on the phone. "What's your hat size?"

"Maybe you think I can't get to you," the man said. "But I can get to you, man. I don't care who you are, I'll get to you. The brothers will get to you."

"Well, there's no need to go to California. You know where we live."

"For God's sake," Grace said.

"Fuckin' right," the man on the telephone said. "Fuckin' right I know."

"Come on over," Elliot said.

"How's that?" the man on the phone asked.

"I said come on over. We'll talk about space travel. Comets and stuff. We'll talk astral projection. The moons of Jupiter."

"You're making a mistake, fucker."

"Come on over," Elliot insisted. "Bring your fat wife and your beat-up kid. Don't be embarrassed if your head's a little small."

The telephone was full of music and shouting. Elliot held it away from his ear.

"Good work," Grace said to him when he had replaced the receiver.

"I hope he comes," Elliot said. "I'll pop him."

He went carefully down the cellar stairs, switched on the overhead light and began searching among the spiderwebbed shadows and fouled fishing line for his shotgun. It took him fifteen minutes to find it and his cleaning case. While he was still downstairs, he heard the telephone ring again and his wife answer it. He came upstairs and spread his shooting gear across the kitchen table. "Was that him?"

She nodded wearily. "He called back to play us the chain saw."

"I've heard that melody before," Elliot said.

He assembled his cleaning rod and swabbed out the shotgun barrel. Grace watched him, a hand to her forehead. "God," she said. "What have I done? I'm so drunk."

"Most of the time," Elliot said, sighting down the barrel, "I'm helpless in the face of human misery. Tonight I'm ready to reach out."

"I'm finished," Grace said. "I'm through, Chas. I mean it."

Elliot rammed three red shells into the shotgun and pumped one forward into the breech with a satisfying report. "Me, I'm ready for some radical problem-solving. I'm going to spray that no-neck Slovak all over the yard."

"He isn't a Slovak," Grace said. She stood in the middle of the kitchen with her eyes closed. Her face was chalk white.

"What do you mean?" Elliot demanded. "Certainly he's a Slovak."

"No he's not," Grace said.

"Fuck him anyway. I don't care what he is. I'll grease his ass."

He took a handful of deer shells from the box and stuffed them in his jacket pockets.

"I'm not going to stay with you, Chas. Do you understand me?"

Elliot walked to the window and peered out at his driveway. "He won't be alone. They travel in packs."

"For God's sake!" Grace cried, and in the next instant bolted for the downstairs bathroom. Elliot went out, turned off the porch light and switched on a spotlight over the barn door. Back inside, he could hear Grace in the toilet being sick. He turned off the light in the kitchen.

He was still standing by the window when she came up behind him. It seemed strange and fateful to be standing in the dark near her, holding the shotgun. He felt ready for anything.

"I can't leave you alone down here drunk with a loaded shotgun," she said. "How can I?"

"Go upstairs," he said.

"If I went upstairs it would mean I didn't care what happened. Do you understand? If I go it means I don't care anymore. Understand?"

"Stop asking me if I understand," Elliot said. "I understand fine."

"I can't think," she said in a sick voice. "Maybe I don't care. I don't know. I'm going upstairs."

"Good," Elliot said.

When she was upstairs, Elliot took his shotgun and the whiskey into the dark living room and sat down in an armchair beside one of the lace-curtained windows. The powerful barn light illuminated the length of his driveway and the whole of the back yard. From the window at which he sat, he commanded a view of several miles in the direction of East Ilford. The two-lane blacktop road that ran there was the only one along which an enemy could pass.

He drank and watched the snow, toying with the safety of his 12-gauge Remington. He felt neither anxious nor angry now but only impatient to be done with whatever the night would bring. Drunkenness and the silent rhythm of the falling snow combined to make him feel outside of time and syntax.

Sitting in the dark room, he found himself confronting

Blankenship's dream. He saw the bunkers and wire of some long-lost perimeter. The rank smell of night came back to him, the dread evening and quick dusk, the mysteries of outer darkness: fear, combat and death. Enervated by liquor, he began to cry. Elliot was sympathetic with other people's tears but ashamed of his own. He thought of his own tears as childish and excremental. He stifled whatever it was that had started them.

Now his whiskey tasted thin as water. Beyond the lightly frosted glass, illuminated snowflakes spun and settled sleepily on weighted pine boughs. He had found a life beyond the war after all, but in it he was still sitting in darkness, armed, enraged, waiting.

His eyes grew heavy as the snow came down. He felt as though he could be drawn up into the storm and he began to imagine that. He imagined his life with all its artifacts and appetites easing up the spout into white oblivion, everything obviated and foreclosed. He thought maybe he could go for that.

When he awakened, his left hand had gone numb against the trigger guard of his shotgun. The living room was full of pale, delicate light. He looked outside and saw that the storm was done with and the sky radiant and cloudless. The sun was still below the horizon.

Slowly Elliot got to his feet. The throbbing poison in his limbs served to remind him of the state of things. He finished the glass of whiskey on the windowsill beside his easy chair. Then he went to the hall closet to get a ski jacket, shouldered his shotgun and went outside.

There were two cleared acres behind his house; beyond them a trail descended into a hollow of pine forest and frozen swamp. Across the hollow, white pastures stretched to the ridge line, lambent under the lightening sky. A line of skeletal elms weighted with snow marked the course of frozen Shawmut Brook.

He found a pair of ski goggles in a jacket pocket and put them on and set out toward the tree line, gripping the shotgun, step by careful step in the knee-deep snow. Two raucous crows wheeled high overhead, their cries exploding the morning's silence. When the sun came over the ridge, he stood where he was and took in a deep breath. The risen sun warmed his face and he closed his eyes. It was windless and very cold.

Only after he had stood there for a while did he realize how tired he had become. The weight of the gun taxed him. It seemed infinitely wearying to contemplate another single step in the snow. He opened his eyes and closed them again. With sunup the world had gone blazing blue and white, and even with his tinted goggles its whiteness dazzled him and made his head ache. Behind his eyes, the hypnagogic patterns formed a monsoon-heavy tropical sky. He yawned. More than anything, he wanted to lie down in the soft, pure snow. If he could do that, he was certain he could go to sleep at once.

He stood in the middle of the field and listened to the crows. Fear, anger and sleep were the three primary conditions of life. He had learned that over there. Once he had thought fear the worst, but he had learned that the worst was anger. Nothing could fix it, neither alcohol nor medicine. It was a worm. It left him no peace. Sleep was the best.

He opened his eyes and pushed on until he came to the brow that overlooked the swamp. Just below, gliding along among the frozen cattails and bare scrub maple, was a man on skis. Elliot stopped to watch the man approach.

The skier's face was concealed by a red and blue ski mask. He wore snow goggles, a blue jumpsuit and a red woollen Norwegian hat. As he came, he leaned into the turns of the trail, moving silently and gracefully along. At the foot of the slope on which Elliot stood, the man looked up, saw him and slid to a halt. The man stood staring at him for a moment and then began to herringbone up the slope. In no time at all the skier stood no more than ten feet away, removing his goggles, and inside the woollen mask Elliot recognized the clear blue eyes of his neighbor, Professor Loyall Anderson. The shotgun Elliot was carrying seemed to grow heavier. He yawned and shook his head, trying unsuccessfully to clear it. The sight of Anderson's eyes gave him a little thrill of revulsion.

"What are you after?" the young professor asked him, nodding toward the shotgun Elliot was cradling.

"Whatever there is," Elliot said.

Anderson took a quick look at the distant pasture behind him and then turned back to Elliot. The mouth hole of the professor's mask filled with teeth. Elliot thought that Anderson's teeth were quite as he had imagined them earlier. "Well, Polonski's cows are locked up," the professor said. "So they at least are safe."

Elliot realized that the professor had made a joke and was smiling. "Yes," he agreed.

Professor Anderson and his wife had been the moving force behind an initiative to outlaw the discharge of firearms within the boundaries of East Ilford Township. The initiative had been defeated, because East Ilford was not that kind of town.

"I think I'll go over by the river," Elliot said. He said it only to have something to say, to fill the silence before Anderson spoke again. He was afraid of what Anderson might say to him and of what might happen.

"You know," Anderson said, "that's all bird sanctuary over there now."

"Sure," Elliot agreed.

Outfitted as he was, the professor attracted Elliot's anger in an elemental manner. The mask made him appear a kind of doll, a kachina figure or a marionette. His eyes and mouth, all on their own, were disagreeable.

Elliot began to wonder if Anderson could smell the whiskey on his breath. He pushed the little red bull's-eye safety button on his gun to Off.

"Seriously," Anderson said, "I'm always having to run hunters out of there. Some people don't understand the word 'posted.'"

"I would never do that," Elliot said. "I would be afraid."

Anderson nodded his head. He seemed to be laughing. "Would you?" he asked Elliot merrily.

In imagination, Elliot rested the tip of his shotgun barrel against Anderson's smiling teeth. If he fired a load of deer shot into them, he thought, they might make a noise like broken china. "Yes," Elliot said. "I wouldn't know who they were or where they'd been. They might resent my being alive. Telling them where they could shoot and where not."

Anderson's teeth remained in place. "That's pretty strange," he said. "I mean, to talk about resenting someone for being alive."

"It's all relative," Elliot said. "They might think, 'Why should he be alive when some brother of mine isn't?' Or they might think, 'Why should he be alive when I'm not?'"

"Oh," Anderson said.

"You see?" Elliot said. Facing Anderson, he took a long step backward. "All relative."

"Yes," Anderson said.

"That's so often true, isn't it?" Elliot asked. "Values are often relative."

"Yes," Anderson said. Elliot was relieved to see that he had stopped smiling.

"I've hardly slept, you know," Elliot told Professor Anderson. "Hardly at all. All night. I've been drinking."

"Oh," Anderson said. He licked his lips in the mouth of the mask. "You should get some rest."

"You're right," Elliot said.

"Well," Anderson said, "got to go now."

Elliot thought he sounded a little thick in the tongue. A little slow in the jaw.

"It's a nice day," Elliot said, wanting now to be agreeable.

"It's great," Anderson said, shuffling on his skis.

"Have a nice day," Elliot said.

"Yes," Anderson said, and pushed off.

Elliot rested the shotgun across his shoulders and watched Anderson withdraw through the frozen swamp. It was in fact a nice day, but Elliot took no comfort in the weather. He missed night and the falling snow.

As he walked back toward his house, he realized that now there would be whole days to get through, running before the antic energy of whiskey. The whiskey would drive him until he dropped. He shook his head in regret. "It's a revolution," he said aloud. He imagined himself talking to his wife.

Getting drunk was an insurrection, a revolution — a bad one. There would be outsize bogus emotions. There would be petty moral blackmail and cheap remorse. He had said dreadful things to his wife. He had bullied Anderson with his violence and unhappiness, and Anderson would not forgive him. There would be damn little justice and no mercy.

Nearly to the house, he was startled by the desperate feathered drumming of a pheasant's rush. He froze, and out of instinct brought the gun up in the direction of the sound. When he saw the bird break from its cover and take wing, he tracked it, took a breath and fired once. The bird was a little flash of opulent color against the bright blue sky. Elliot felt himself flying for a moment. The shot missed.

Lowering the gun, he remembered the deer shells he had loaded. A hit with the concentrated shot would have pulverized the bird, and he was glad he had missed. He wished no harm to any creature. Then he thought of himself wishing no harm to any creature and began to feel fond and sorry for himself. As soon as he grew aware of the emotion he was indulging, he suppressed it. Pissing and moaning, mourning and weeping, that was the nature of the drug.

The shot echoed from the distant hills. Smoke hung in the air. He turned and looked behind him and saw, far away across the pasture, the tiny blue and red figure of Professor Anderson motionless against the snow. Then Elliot turned again toward his house and took a few labored steps and looked up to see his wife at the bedroom window. She stood perfectly still, and the morning sun lit her nakedness. He stopped where he was. She had heard the shot and run to the window. What had she thought to see? Burnt rags and blood on the snow. How relieved was she now? How disappointed?

Elliot thought he could feel his wife trembling at the window. She was hugging herself. Her hands clasped her shoulders. Elliot took his snow goggles off and shaded his eyes with his hand. He stood in the field staring.

The length of the gun was between them, he thought. Somehow she had got out in front of it, to the wrong side of the wire. If he looked long enough he would find everything out there. He would find himself down the sight.

How beautiful she is, he thought. The effect was striking. The window was so clear because he had washed it himself, with vinegar. At the best of times he was a difficult, fussy man.

Elliot began to hope for forgiveness. He leaned the shotgun on his forearm and raised his left hand and waved to her. Show a hand, he thought. Please just show a hand.

He was cold, but it had got light. He wanted no more than the gesture. It seemed to him that he could build another day on it. Another day was all you needed. He raised his hand higher and waited.

UNDER THE PITONS

➤

ALL THE PREVIOUS DAY, they had been tacking up from the Grenadines, bound for Martinique to return the boat and take leave of Freycinet. Blessington was trying to forget the anxieties of the deal, the stink of menace, the sick ache behind the eyes. It was dreadful to have to smoke with the St. Vincentian dealers, stone killers who liked to operate from behind a thin film of fear. But the Frenchman was tough.

Off Dark Head there was a near thing with a barge under tow. Blessington, stoned at the wheel, his glass of straight Demerara beside the binnacle, had calmly watched a dimly lighted tug struggle past on a parallel course at a distance of a mile or so. The moon was newly risen, out of sight behind the island's mountains, silvering the line of the lower slopes. A haze of starlight left the sea in darkness, black as the pit, now and then flashing phosphorescence. They were at least ten miles offshore.

With his mainsail beginning to luff, he had steered the big ketch a little farther off the wind, gliding toward the trail of living light in the tug's wake. Only in the last second did the dime drop; he took a quick look over his shoulder. And of course there came the barge against the moon-traced mountains, a big black homicidal juggernaut, unmarked and utterly

unlighted, bearing down on them. Blessington swore and spun
the wheel like Ezekiel, as hard to port as it went, thinking that
if his keel was over the cable nothing would save them, that
360 degrees of helm or horizon would be less than enough to
escape by.

Then everything not secured came crashing down on everything else, the tables and chairs on the afterdeck went over,
plates and bottles smashed, whatever was breakable immediately broke. The boat, the *Sans Regret*, fell off the wind like a
comedian and flapped into a flying jibe. A couple of yards to
starboard the big barge raced past like a silent freight train,
betrayed only by the slap of its hull against the waves. It might
have been no more than the wind, for all you could hear of it.
When it was safely gone, the day's fear welled up again and
gagged him.

The Frenchman ran out on deck cursing and looked to the
cockpit, where Blessington had the helm. His hair was cut close
to his skull. He showed his teeth in the mast light. He was
brushing his shorts; something had spilled in his lap.

"*Qu'est-ce que c'est là?*" he demanded of Blessington. Blessington pointed into the darkness where the barge had disappeared. The Frenchman knew only enough of the ocean to fear
the people on it. "*Quel cul!*" he said savagely. "Who is it?" He
was afraid of the Coast Guard and of pirates.

"We just missed being sunk by a barge. No lights. Submerged
cable. It's OK now."

"Fuck," said the Frenchman, Freycinet. "Why are you stopping?"

"Stopping?" It took a moment to realize that Freycinet was
under the impression that because the boat had lost its forward
motion they were stopping, as though he had applied a brake.
Freycinet had been around boats long enough to know better.
He must be out of his mind, Blessington thought.

"I'm not stopping, Honoré. We're all right."

"I bust my fucking ass below," said Freycinet. "Marie fall out of bed."

Tough shit, thought Blessington. Be thankful you're not treading water in the splinters of your stupidly named boat. "Sorry, man," he said.

Sans Regret, with its fatal echoes of Piaf. The Americans might be culturally deprived, Blessington thought, but surely every cutter in the Yankee Coast Guard would have the sense to board that one. And the cabin stank of the resiny ganja they had stashed, along with the blow, under the cabin sole. No amount of roach spray or air freshener could cut it. The space would probably smell of dope forever.

Freycinet went below without further complaint, missing in his ignorance the opportunity to abuse Blessington at length. It had been Blessington's fault they had not seen the barge sooner, stoned and drunk as he was. He should have looked for it as soon as the tug went by. To stay awake through the night he had taken crystal and his peripheral vision was flashing him little mongoose darts, shooting stars composed of random light. Off the north shore of St. Vincent, the winds were murder.

Just before sunrise, he saw the Pitons rising from the sea off the starboard bow, the southwest coast of St. Lucia. Against the pink sky, the two peaks looked like a single mountain. It was hard to take them for anything but a good omen. As the sudden dawn caught fire, they turned green with hope. So many hearts, he thought, must have lifted at the sight of them.

To Blessington, they looked like the beginning of home free. Or at least free. Martinique was the next island up, where they could return the boat and Blessington could take his portion and be off to America on his student visa. He had a letter of acceptance from a hotel management school in Florida but his dream was to open a restaurant in the Keys.

He took another deep draft of the rum to cut the continuing anxieties. The first sunlight raised a sweat on him, so he took his shirt off and put on his baseball hat. Florida Marlins.

Freycinet came out on deck while he was having a drink.

"You're a drunk Irish man," Freycinet told him.

"That I'm not," said Blessington. It seemed to him no matter how much he drank he would never be drunk again. The three Vincentians had sobered him for life. He had been sitting on the porch of the guesthouse on Canouan when they walked up. They had approached like panthers — no metaphor, no politics intended. Their every move was a dark roll of musculature, balanced and wary. They were very big men with square scarred faces. Blessington had been reclining, tilted backward in a cane chair with his feet on the porch rail, when they came up to him.

"Frenchy?" one had asked very softly.

Blessington had learned the way of hard men back in Ireland and thought he could deal with them. He had been careful to maintain his relaxed position.

"I know the man you mean, sir," he had said. "But I'm not him, see. You'll have to wait."

At Blessington's innocuous words they had tensed in every fiber, although you had to be looking right at them to appreciate the physics of it. They drew themselves up around their hidden weaponry behind a silent, drug-glazed wall of suspicion that looked impermeable to reason. They were zombies, without mercy, and he, Blessington, was wasting their time. He resolved to count to thirty, but at the count of ten he took his feet down off the rail.

Freycinet turned and shaded his eyes and looked toward the St. Lucia coast. The Pitons delighted him.

"*Ah là. C'est les Pitons, n'est-ce pas?*"

"*Oui*," said Blessington. "*Les Pitons.*" They had gone south in darkness and Freycinet had never seen them before.

The wind shifted to its regular quarter and he had a hard time tacking level with the island. The two women came out on deck. Freycinet's Marie was blond and very young. She came from Normandy, and she had been a waitress in the bistro outside Fort-de-France where Freycinet and Blessington cooked. Sometimes she seemed so sunny and innocent that it was hard to connect her with a hood like Freycinet. At other times she seemed very knowing indeed. It was hard to tell, she was so often stoned.

Gillian was an American from Texas. She had a hard, thin face with a prominent nose and a big jaw. Her father, Blessington imagined, was one of those Texans, a tough, loud man who cursed the Mexicans. She was extremely tall and rather thin, with long legs. Her slenderness and height and interesting face had taken her into modeling, to Paris and Milan. In contrast, she had muscular thighs and a big derriere, which, if it distressed the couturiers, made her more desirable. She was Blessington's designated girlfriend on the trip but they rarely made love because, influenced by the others, he had taken an early dislike to her. He supposed she knew it.

"Oh, wow," she said in her Texas voice, "look at those pretty mountains."

It was exactly the kind of American comment that made the others all despise and imitate her — even Marie, who had no English at all. Gillian had come on deck stark naked and each of them, the Occitan Freycinet, Norman Marie and Irish Blessington, felt scornful and slightly offended. Anyone else might have been forgiven. They had decided she was a type and she could do no right.

Back on Canouan, Gillian had conceived a lust for one of the dealers. At first, when everyone smoked in the safe house, they had paid no attention to the women. The deal was repeated to everyone's satisfaction. As the dealers gave forth their odor of menace Marie had skillfully disappeared herself in plain view. But Gillian, to Blessington's humiliation and alarm, had put out a ray and one of the men had called her on it.

Madness. In a situation so volatile, so bloody *fraught*. But she was full of lusts, was Texan Gillian, and physically courageous too. He noticed she whined less than the others, in spite of her irritating accent. It had ended with her following the big St. Vincentian to her guesthouse room, walking ten paces behind with her eyes down, making herself a prisoner, a lamb for the slaughter.

For a while Blessington had thought she would have to do all three of them but it had been only the one, Nigel. Nigel had returned her to Blessington in a grim little ceremony, holding her with the chain of her shark's-tooth necklace twisted tight around her neck.

"Wan' have she back, mon?"

Leaving Blessington with the problem of how to react. The big bastard was fucking welcome to her, but of course it would have been tactless to say so. Should he protest and get everyone killed? Or should he be complacent and be thought a pussy and possibly achieve the same result? It was hard to find a middle ground but Blessington found one, a tacit, ironic posture, fashioned of silences and body language. The Irish had been a subject race too, after all.

"I gon' to make you a present, mon. Give you little pink piggy back. Goodness of my ha'art."

So saying, Nigel had put his huge busted-knuckle hand against her pale hard face and she had looked down submissively, trembling a little, knowing not to smile. Afterward, she was very cool about it. Nigel had given her a Rasta bracelet, beads in the red, yellow and green colors of Ras Tafari.

"Think I'm a pink piggy, Liam?"

He had not been remotely amused and he had told her so.

So she had walked on ahead laughing and put her palms

together and looked up to the sky and said, "Oh, my Lord!" And then glanced at him and wiped the smile off her face. Plainly she'd enjoyed it, all of it. She wore the bracelet constantly.

Now she leaned on her elbows against the chart table with her bare bum thrust out, turning the bracelet with the long, bony fingers of her right hand. Though often on deck, she seemed never to burn or tan. A pale child of night was Gillian.

"What island you say that was?" she asked.

"It's St. Lucia," Blessington told her. "The mountains are called the Pitons."

"The Pee-tuns? Does that mean something cool in French?" She turned to Blessington, then to Freycinet. "Does it, Honoré?"

Freycinet made an unpleasant, ratty face. He was ugly as cat shit, Blessington thought, something Gillian doubtless appreciated. He had huge soulful brown eyes and a pointed nose like a puppet's. His grim haircut showed the flattened shape of his skull.

"It means stakes," Blessington said.

"Steaks? Like . . ."

"Sticks," said Blessington. "Rods. Palings."

"Oh," she said, "stakes. Like Joan of Arc got burned at, right?"

Freycinet's mouth fell open. Marie laughed loudly. Gillian looked slyly at Blessington.

"Honoré," she said. "*Tu es un dindon.* You're a *dindon,* man. I'm shitting you. I understand French fine."

It had become amusing to watch her tease and confound Freycinet. Dangerous work and she did it cleverly, leaving the Frenchman to marvel at the depths of her stupidity until paranoia infected his own self-confidence. During the trip back, Blessington thought he might be starting to see the point of her.

"I mean, I worked the Paris openings for five years straight. I told you that."

Drunk and stoned as the rest of them, Gillian eventually withdrew from the ascending spring sun. Marie went down after her. Freycinet's pointed nose was out of joint.

"You hear what she say?" he asked Blessington. "That she speak French all the time? What the fuck? Because she said before, '*Non*, I don't speak it.' Now she's speaking it."

"Ah, she's drunk, Honoré. She's just a bimbo."

"I 'ope so, eh?" said Freycinet. He looked at the afterdeck to be sure she was out of earshot. "Because . . . because what if she setting us up? All these time, eh? If she's *agent*. Or she's informer? A grass?"

Blessington pondered it deeply. Like the rest of them he had thought her no more than a fatuous, if perverse, American. Now, the way she laughed at them, he was not at all sure.

"I thought she came with you. Did she put money up?"

Freycinet puffed out his hollow cheeks and shrugged.

"She came to me from Lavigerie," he said. The man who called himself Lavigerie was a French Israeli of North African origin, a hustler in Fort-de-France. "She put in money, *oui*. The same as everyone."

They had all pooled their money for the boat and to pay the Vincentians. Blessington had invested twenty thousand dollars, partly his savings from the bistro, partly borrowed from his sister and her husband in Providence. He expected to make it back many times and pay them off with interest.

"Twenty thousand?"

"Yes. Twenty."

"Well, even the Americans wouldn't spend twenty thousand dollars to catch us," he told Honoré. "We're too small. And it isn't how they work."

"Now I think I don't trust her, eh?" said Freycinet. He squinted into the sun. The Pitons, no closer, seemed to displease him now. "She's a bitch, *non*?"

"I think she's all right," Blessington said. "I really do."

And for the most part he did. In any case he had decided to, because an eruption of hard-core, coke-and-speed-headed paranoia could destroy them all. It had done so to many others. Missing boats sometimes turned up on the mangrove shore of some remote island, the hulls blistered with bullet holes, cabins attended by unimaginable swarms of flies. Inside, *tableaux morts* not to be forgotten by the unlucky discoverer. Strong-stomached photographers recorded the *tableaux* for the DEA's files, where they were stamped NOT TO BE DESTROYED, HISTORIC INTEREST. The agency took a certain satisfaction. Blessington knew all this from his sister and her husband in Providence.

Now they were almost back to Martinique and Blessington wanted intensely not to die at sea. In the worst of times, he grew frightened to the point of utter despair. It had been, he realized at such times, a terrible mistake. He gave up on the money. He would settle for just living, for living even in prison in France or America. Or at least for not dying on that horrible bright blue ocean, aboard the *Sans Regret*.

"Yeah," he told Freycinet. "Hell, I wouldn't worry about her. Just a bimbo."

All morning they tacked for the Pitons. Around noon, a great crown of puffy cloud settled around Gros Piton and they were close enough to distinguish the two peaks one from the other. Freycinet refused to go below. His presence was so unpleasant that Blessington felt like weeping, knocking him unconscious, throwing him overboard or jumping over himself. But the Frenchman remained in the cockpit though he never offered to spell Blessington at the wheel. The man drove Blessington to drink. He poured more Demerara and dipped his finger in the bag of crystal. A pulse fluttered under his collarbone, fear, speed.

Eventually Freycinet went below. After half an hour, Gillian came topside, clothed this time, in cutoffs and a halter. The sea had picked up and she nearly lost her balance on the ladder.

"Steady," said Blessington.

"Want a roofie, Liam?"

He laughed. "A roofie? What's that? Some kind of . . ."

Gillian finished the thought he had been too much of a prude to articulate.

"Some kind of blowjob? Some kind of sex technique? No, dear, it's a medication."

"I'm on watch."

She laughed at him. "You're shitfaced is what you are."

"You know," Blessington said, "you ought not to tease Honoré. You'll make him paranoid."

"He's a asshole. As we say back home."

"That may be. But he's a very mercurial fella. I used to work with him."

"Mercurial? If you know he's so mercurial how come you brought him?"

"I didn't bring him," Blessington said. "He brought me. For my vaunted seamanship. And I came for the money. How about you?"

"I came on account of having my brains in my ass," she said, shaking her backside. "My talent too. Did you know I was a barrel racer? I play polo too. English or western, man, you name it."

"English or western?" Blessington asked.

"Forget it," she said. She frowned at him, smiled, frowned again. "You seem, well, scared."

"Ah," said Blessington, "scared? Yes, I am. Somewhat."

"I don't give a shit," she said.

"You don't?"

"You heard me," she said. "I don't care what happens. Why should I? Me with my talent in my ass. Where do I come in?"

"You shouldn't talk that way," Blessington said.

"Fuck you. You afraid I'll make trouble? I assure you I could make trouble like you wouldn't believe."

"I don't doubt it," Blessington said. He kept his eyes on the Pitons. His terror, he thought, probably encouraged her.

"Just between you and me, Liam, I have no fear of dying. I would just as soon be out here on this boat now as in my little comfy bed with my stuffed animals. I would just as soon be dead."

He took another sip of rum to wet his pipes for speech. "Why did you put the money in, then? Weren't you looking for a score?"

"I don't care about money," she said. "I thought it would be a kick. I thought it would be radical. But it's just another exercise in how everything sucks."

"Well," said Blessington, "you're right there."

She looked off at the twin mountains.

"They don't seem a bit closer than they did this morning."

"No. It's an upwind passage. Have to tack forever."

"You know what Nigel told me back in Canouan?"

"No," Blessington said.

"He told me not to worry about understanding things. He said understanding was weak and lame. He said you got to *overstand* things." She hauled herself and did the voice of a big St. Vincentian man saddling up a white bitch for the night, laying down wisdom. "You got to *overstand* it. *Overstand* it, right? Funny, huh."

"Maybe there's something in it," said Blessington.

"Rasta lore," she said. "Could be, man."

"Anyway, never despise what the natives tell you, that's what my aunt used to say. Even in America."

"And what was your aunt? A dope dealer?"

"She was a nun," Blessington said. "A missionary."

For a while Gillian sunned herself on the foredeck, halter off.

But the sun became too strong and she crawled back to the cockpit.

"You ever think about how it is in this part of the world?" she asked him. "The Caribbean and around it? It's all suckin' stuff they got. Suckin' stuff, all goodies and no nourishment."

"What do you mean?"

"It's all turn-ons and illusion," she said. "Don't you think? Like coffee." She numbered items on the long fingers of her left hand. "Tobacco. Emeralds. Sugar. Cocaine. Ganja. It's all stuff you don't need. Isn't even good for you. Perks and pick-me-ups and pogy bait. Always has been."

"You're right," Blessington said. "Things people kill for."

"Overpriced. Put together by slaves and peons. Piggy stuff. For pink piggies."

"I hadn't thought of it," he said. He looked over at her. She had raised a fist to her pretty mouth. "You're clever, Gillian."

"You don't even like me," she said.

"Yes I do."

"Don't you dare bullshit me. I said you don't."

"Well," Blessington said, "to tell you the truth, at first I didn't. But now I do."

"Oh, yeah? Why?"

Blessington considered before speaking. The contrary wind was picking up and there were reefs at the south end of the island. Some kind of monster tide was running against them too.

"Because you're intelligent. I hadn't realized that. You had me fooled, see? Now I think you're amusing."

"Amusing?" She seemed more surprised than angry.

"You really are so bloody clever," he said, finishing the glass of rum. "When we're together I like it. You're not a cop, are you? Anything like that?"

"You only wish," she said. "How about you?"

"Me? I'm Irish, for Christ's sake."

"Is that like not being real?"

"Well," he said, "a little. In many cases."

"You are scared," she said. "You're scared of everything. Scared of me."

"Holy Christ," said Blessington, "you're as bad as Honoré. Look, Gillian, I'm a chef, not a pirate. I never claimed otherwise. Of course I'm scared."

She made him no answer.

"But not of you," he said. "No. Not anymore. I like you here. You're company."

"Am I?" she asked. "Do you? Would you marry me?"

"Hey," said Blessington. "Tomorrow."

Freycinet came up on deck, looked at the Pitons, then at Blessington and Gillian in the cockpit.

"*Merde,*" he said. "Far away still. What's going on?"

"We're getting there," Blessington said. "We're closer now than we look."

"Aren't the mountains pretty, Honoré?" Gillian asked. "Don't you wish we could climb one?"

Freycinet ignored her. "How long?" he asked Blessington.

"To Martinique? Tomorrow sometime, I guess."

"How long before we're off les Pitons?"

"Oh," Blessington said, "just a few hours. Well before dark so we'll have a view. Better steer clear, though."

"Marie is sick."

"Poor puppy," Gillian said. "Probably all that bug spray. Broth's the thing. Don't you think, Liam?"

"Ya, it's kicking up," Blessington said. "There's a current running and a pretty stiff offshore breeze."

"*Merde,*" said Freycinet again. He went forward along the rail and lay down beside the anchor windlass, peering into the chains.

"He's a cook too," Gillian said, speaking softly. "How come you're not more like him?"

"An accident of birth," Blessington said.

"If we were married," she said, "you wouldn't have to skip on your visa."

"Ah," said Blessington, "don't think it hasn't occurred to me. Nice to be a legal resident."

"Legal my ass," she said.

Freycinet suddenly turned and watched them. He showed them the squint, the bared canines.

"What you're talking about, you two? About me, eh?"

"Damn, Honoré!" Gillian said. "He was just proposing." When he had turned around again she spoke between her teeth. "Shithead is into the blow. He keeps prying up the sole. Cures Marie's mal de mer. Keeps him on his toes."

"God save us," said Blessington. Leaning his elbow on the helm, he took Gillian's right hand and put it to her forehead, her left shoulder and then her right one, walking her through the sign of the cross. "Pray for us like a good girl."

Gillian made the sign again by herself. "Shit," she said, "now I feel a lot better. No, really," she said when he laughed, "I do. I'm ᴇᴇ ᵗ do it all the time now. Instead of chanting *Om* or *Nam myoho renge kyo*."

They sat and watched the peaks grow closer, though the contrary current increased.

"When this is over," Blessington said, "maybe we ought to stay friends."

"If we're still alive," she said, "we might hang out together. We could go to your restaurant in the Keys."

"That's what we'll do," he said. "I'll make you a sous-chef."

"I'll wait tables."

"No, no. Not you."

"But we won't be alive," she said.

"But if we are."

"If we are," she said, "we'll stay together." She looked at him sway beside the wheel. "You better not be shitting me."

"I wouldn't. I think it was meant to be."

"Meant to be? You're putting me on."

"Don't make me weigh my words, Gillian. I want to say what occurs to me."

"Right," she said, touching him. "When we're together you can say any damn thing."

The green mountains, in the full richness of afternoon, rose above them. Blessington had a look at the chart to check the location of the offshore reefs. He began steering to another quarter, away from the tip of the island.

Gillian sat on a locker with her arms around his neck, leaning against his back. She smelled of sweat and patchouli.

"I've never been with anyone as beautiful as you, Gillian."

He saw she had gone to sleep. He disengaged her arms and helped her lie flat on the locker in the shifting shade of the mainsail. Life is a dream, he thought. Something she knew and I didn't.

I love her, Blessington thought. She encourages me. The shadow of the peaks spread over the water.

Freycinet came out on deck and called up to him.

"Liam! We're to stop here. Off les Pitons."

"We can't," Blessington said, though it was tempting. He was so tired.

"We have to stop. We can anchor, yes? Marie is sick. We need to rest. We want to see them."

"We'd have to clear customs," Blessington said. "We'll have bloody cops and boat boys and God knows what else."

He realized at once what an overnight anchorage would entail. All of them up on speed or the cargo, cradling shotguns, peering into the moonlight while they waited for *macheteros* to come on feathered oars and steal their shit and kill them.

"If we anchor," Freycinet said, "if we anchor somewhere, we won't have to clear."

"Yes, yes," Blessington said. "We will, sure. The fucking boat boys will find us. If we don't hire them or buy something they'll turn us in." He picked up the cruising guide and waved it in the air. "It says right here you have to clear customs in Soufrière."

"We'll wait until they have close," said Freycinet.

"Shit," said Blessington desperately, "we'll be fined. We'll be boarded."

Freycinet was smiling at him, a broad demented smile of infinitely self-assured contempt. Cocaine. He felt Gillian put her arm around his leg from behind.

"*Écoutez*, Liam. *Écoutez bien*. We going to stop, man. We going to stop where I say."

He turned laughing into the wind, gripping a stay.

"What did I tell you," Gillian said softly. "You won't have to marry me after all. 'Cause we're dead, baby."

"I don't accept that," Blessington said. "Take the wheel," he told her.

Referring to the charts and the cruising guide, he could find no anchorage that looked as though it would be out of the wind and that was not close inshore. The only possibility was a shallow reef, near the south tip, sometimes favored by snorkeling trips, nearly three miles off the Pitons. It was in the lee of the huge peaks, its coral heads as shallow as a single fathom. The chart showed mooring floats; presumably it was forbidden to anchor there for the sake of the coral.

"I beg you to reconsider, Honoré," Blessington said to Freycinet. He cleared his throat. "You're making a mistake."

Freycinet turned back to him with the same smile.

"Eh, Liam. You can leave, man. You know, there's an Irish pub in Soufrière. It's money from your friends in the IRA. You can go there, eh?"

Blessington had no connection whatsoever with the IRA, although he had allowed Freycinet and his friends to believe that, and they had chosen to.

"You can go get drunk there," Freycinet told him and then turned again to look at the island.

He was standing near the bow with his bare toes caressing freeboard, gripping a stay. Blessington and Gillian exchanged looks. In the next instant she threw the wheel, the mainsail boom went crashing across the cabin roofs, the boat lurched to port and heeled hard. For a moment Freycinet was suspended over blank blue water. Blessington clambered up over the cockpit and stood swaying there, hesitating. Then he reached out for Freycinet. The Frenchman swung around the stay like a monkey and knocked him flat. The two of them went sprawling. Freycinet got to his feet in a karate stance, cursing.

"You shit," he said, when his English returned. "Cunt! What?"

"I thought you were going over, Honoré. I thought I'd have to pull you back aboard."

"That's right, Honoré," Gillian said from the cockpit. "You were like a goner. He saved your ass, man."

Freycinet pursed his lips and nodded. "*Bien,*" he said. He climbed down into the cockpit in a brisk, businesslike fashion and slapped Gillian across the face, backhand and forehand, turning her head around each time.

He gave Blessington the wheel, then he took Gillian under the arm and pulled her up out of the cockpit. "Get below! I don't want to fucking see you." He followed her below and Blessington heard him speak briefly to Marie. The young woman began to moan. The Pitons looked close enough to strike with a rock and a rich jungle smell came out on the wind. Freycinet, back on deck, looked as though he was sniffing out menace. A divi-divi bird landed on the boom for a moment and then fluttered away.

"I think I have a place," Blessington said, "if you still insist. A reef."

"A reef, eh?"

"A reef about four thousand meters offshore."

"We could have a swim, *non?*"

"We could, yes."

"But I don't know if I want to swim with you, Liam. I think you try to push me overboard."

"I think I saved your life," Blessington said.

They motored on to the reef with Freycinet standing in the bow to check for bottom as Blessington watched the depth recorder. At ten meters of bottom, they were an arm's length from the single float in view. Blessington cut the engine and came about and then went forward to cleat a line to the float. The float was painted red, yellow and green, Rasta colors like Gillian's bracelet.

It was late afternoon and suddenly dead calm. The protection the Pitons offered from the wind was ideal and the bad current that ran over the reef to the south seemed to divide around these coral heads. A perfect dive site, Blessington thought, and he could not understand why even in June there were not more floats or more boats anchored there. It seemed a steady enough place even for an overnight anchorage, although the cruising guide advised against it because of the dangerous reefs on every side.

The big ketch lay motionless on unruffled water; the float line drifted slack. There was sandy beach and a palm-lined shore across the water. It was a lonely part of the coast, across a jungle mountain track from the island's most remote resort. Through binoculars Blessington could make out a couple of boats hauled up on the strand but no one seemed ready to come out and hustle them. With luck it was too far from shore.

It might be also, he thought, that for metaphysical reasons the *Sans Regret* presented a forbidding aspect. But an aspect that deterred small predators might in time attract big ones.

Marie came up, pale and hollow-eyed, in her bikini. She gave

Blessington a chastising look and lay down on the cushions on the afterdeck. Gillian came up behind her and took a seat on the gear locker behind Blessington.

"The fucker's got no class," she said softly. "See him hit me?"

"Of course. I was next to you."

"Gonna let him get away with that?"

"Well," Blessington said, "for the moment it behooves us to let him feel in charge."

"Behooves us?" she asked. "You say it *behooves* us?"

"That's right."

"Hey, what were you gonna do back there, Liam?" she asked. "Deep-six him?"

"I honestly don't know. He might have fallen."

"I was wondering," she said. "He was wondering too."

Blessington shrugged.

"He's got the overstanding," Gillian said. "We got the under." She looked out at the water and said, "Boat boys."

He looked where she was looking and saw the boat approaching, a speck against the shiny sand. It took a long time for it to cover the distance between the beach and the *Sans Regret.*

There were two boat boys, and they were not boys but men in their thirties, lean and unsmiling. One wore a wool tam-o'-shanter in bright tie-dyed colors. The second looked like an East Indian. His black headband gave him a lascar look.

"You got to pay for dat anchorage, mon," the man in the tam called to them. "Not open to de public widout charge."

"We coming aboard," said the lascar. "We take your papers and passports in for you. You got to clear."

"How much for the use of the float?" Blessington asked.

Now Freycinet appeared in the companionway. He was carrying a big French MAS 36 sniper rifle, pointing it at the men in the boat, showing his pink-edged teeth.

"You get the fuck out of here," he shouted at them. A smell of ganja and vomit seemed to follow him up from the cabin. "Understand?"

The two men did not seem unduly surprised at Freycinet's behavior. Blessington wondered if they could smell the dope as distinctly as he could.

"Fuckin' Frenchman," the man in the tam said. "Think he some shit."

"Why don' you put the piece down, Frenchy?" the East Indian asked. "This ain't no Frenchy island. You got to clear."

"You drift on that reef, Frenchy," the man in the tam said, "you be begging us to take you off."

Freycinet was beside himself with rage. He hated *les nègres* more than any Frenchman Blessington had met in Martinique, which was saying a great deal. He had contained himself during the negotiations on Canouan but now he seemed out of control. Blessington began to wonder if he would shoot the pair of them.

"You fucking monkeys!" he shouted. "You stay away from me, eh? Chimpanzees! I kill you quick . . . *mon*," he added with a sneer.

The men steered their boat carefully over the reef and sat with their outboard idling. They could not stay too long, Blessington thought. Their gas tank was small and it was a long way out against a current.

"Well," he asked Gillian, "who's got the overstanding now?"

"Not Honoré," she said.

A haze of heat and doped lassitude settled over their mooring. Movement was labored, even speech seemed difficult. Blessington and Gillian nodded off on the gear locker. Marie seemed to have lured Freycinet belowdecks. Prior to dozing, Blessington heard her mimic the Frenchman's angry voice and the two of them laughing down in the cabin. The next thing he saw clearly was Marie, in her bikini, standing on the cabin roof, screaming. A rifle blasted and echoed over the still water. Suddenly the slack breeze had a brisk cordite smell and it carried smoke.

Freycinet shouted, holding the hot shotgun.

The boat with the two islanders in it seemed to have managed to come up on them. Now it raced off, headed first out to sea to round the tip of the reef and then curving shoreward to take the inshore current at an angle.

"Everyone all right?" asked Blessington.

"Fucking monkeys!" Freycinet swore.

"Well," Blessington said, watching the boat disappear, "they're gone for now. Maybe," he suggested to Freycinet, "we can have our swim and go too."

Freycinet looked at him blankly as though he had no idea what Blessington was talking about. He nodded vaguely.

After half an hour Marie rose and stood on the bulwark and prepared to dive, arms foremost. When she went, her dive was a good one, straight-backed and nearly splash-free. She performed a single stroke underwater and sped like a bright shaft between the coral heads below and the crystal surface. Then she appeared prettily in the light of day, blinking like a child, shaking her shining hair.

From his place in the bow, Freycinet watched Marie's dive, her underwater career, her pert surfacing. His expression was not affectionate but taut and tight-lipped. The muscles in his neck stood out, his moves were twitchy like a street junkie's. He looked exhausted and angry. The smell of cordite hovered around him.

"He's a shithead and a loser," Gillian said softly to Blessington. She looked not at Freycinet but toward the green mountains. "I thought he was cool. He was so fucking mean — I like respected that. Now we're all gonna die. Well," she said, "goes to show, right?"

"Don't worry," Blessington told her. "I won't leave you."

"Whoa," said Gillian. "All right!" But her enthusiasm was not genuine. She was mocking him.

Blessington forgave her.

Freycinet pointed a finger at Gillian. "Swim!"

"What if I don't wanna?" she asked, already standing up. When he began to swear at her in a hoarse voice she took her clothes off in front of them. Everything but the Rasta bracelet.

"I think I will if no one minds," she said. "Where you want me to swim to, Honoré?"

"Swim to fucking *Amérique*," he said. He laughed as though his mood had improved. "You want her, Liam?"

"People are always asking me that," Blessington said. "What do I have to do?"

"You swim to fucking *Amérique* with her."

Blessington saw Gillian take a couple of pills from her cutoff pocket and swallow them dry.

"I can't swim that far," Blessington said.

"Go as far as you can," said Freycinet.

"How about you?" Gillian said to the Frenchman. "You're the one wanted to stop. So ain't you gonna swim?"

"I don't trust her," Freycinet said to Blessington. "What do you think?"

"She's a beauty," Blessington said. "Don't provoke her."

Gillian measured her beauty against the blue water and dived over the side. A belly full of pills, Blessington thought. But her strokes when she surfaced were strong and defined. She did everything well, he thought. She was good around the boat. She had a pleasant voice for country music. He could imagine her riding, a cowgirl.

"Bimbo, eh?" Freycinet asked. "That's it, eh?"

"Yes," Blessington said. "Texas and all that."

"*Oui*," said Freycinet. "Texas." He yawned. "*Bien*. Have your swim with her. If you want."

Blessington went down into the stinking cabin and put his bathing suit on. Propriety to the last. The mixture of ganja, sick, roach spray and pine scent was asphyxiating. If he survived, he thought, he would never smoke hash again. Never drink rum, never do speed or cocaine, never sail or go where there were palm trees and too many stars overhead. A few fog-shrouded winter constellations would do.

"Tonight I'll cook, eh?" Freycinet said when Blessington came back up. "You can assist me."

"Good plan," said Blessington.

Standing on the bulwark, he looked around the boat. There were no other vessels in sight. Marie was swimming backstroke, describing a safe circle about twenty-five yards out from the boat. Gillian appeared to be headed hard for the open sea. She had reached the edge of the current, where the wind raised small horsetails from the rushing water.

If Freycinet was planning to leave them in the water, Blessington wondered, would he leave Marie with them? It would all be a bad idea, because Freycinet was not a skilled sailor. And there was a possibility of their being picked up right here or even of their making it to shore, although that seemed most unlikely. On the other hand, he had discovered that Freycinet's ideas were often impulses, usually bad ones. It was his recklessness that had made him appear so capably in charge, and that was as true in the kitchen as it was on the Raging Main. He had been a reckless cook.

Besides, there were a thousand dark possibilities on that awful ocean. That he had arranged to be met at sea off Martinique, that there had been some betrayal in the works throughout. Possibly involving Lavigerie or someone else in Fort-de-France.

"Yes," said Blessington. "There's time to unfreeze the grouper."

He looked at the miles of ocean between the boat and the

beach at the foot of the mountains. Far off to the right he could see white water, the current running swiftly over the top of a reef that extended southwesterly, at a 45-degree angle to the beach. Beyond the reef was a sandspit where the island tapered to its narrow southern end. On their left, the base of the mountains extended to the edge of the sea, forming a rock wall against which the waves broke. According to the charts, the wall plunged to a depth of ten fathoms, and the ocean concealed a network of submarine caves and grottoes in the volcanic rock of which the Pitons were composed. Across the towering ridge, completely out of sight, was the celebrated resort.

"I'll take it out of the freezer," Blessington said.

A swimmer would have to contrive to make land somewhere between the rock wall to the north and the reef and sandspit on the right. There would be easy swimming at first, through the windless afternoon, and a swimmer would not feel any current for the first mile or so. The last part of the swim would be partly against a brisk current, and possibly against the tide. The final mile would seem much farther. For the moment, wind was not in evidence. The current might be counted on to lessen as one drew closer to shore. If only one could swim across it in time.

"It's all right," said Freycinet. "I'll do it. Have your swim."

Beyond that, there was the possibility of big sharks so far out. They might be attracted by the effort of desperation. Blessington, exhausted and dehydrated, was in no mood for swimming miles. Freycinet would not leave them there, off the Pitons, he told himself. It was practically in sight of land. He would be risking too much — witnesses, their survival. If he meant to deep-six them he would try to strike at sea.

Stoned and frightened as he was, he could not make sense of it, regain his perspective. He took a swig from a plastic bottle of warm Evian water, dropped his towel and jumped overboard.

The water felt good, slightly cool. He could relax against it and slow the beating of his heart. It seemed to cleanse him of the cabin stink. He was at home in the water, he thought. Marie was frolicking like a mermaid, now close to the boat. Gillian had turned back and was swimming toward him. Her stroke still looked strong and accomplished; he set out to intercept her course.

They met over a field of elkhorn coral. Some of the formations were so close to the surface that their feet, treading water, brushed the velvety skin of algae over the sharp prongs.

"How are you?" Blessington asked her.

She had a lupine smile. She was laughing, looking at the boat. Her eyes appeared unfocused, the black pupils huge under the blue glare of afternoon and its shimmering crystal reflection. She breathed in hungry swallows. Her face was raw and swollen where Freycinet had hit her.

"Look at that asshole," she said, gasping.

Freycinet was standing on deck talking to Marie, who was in the water ten feet away. He held a mask and snorkel in one hand and a pair of swim fins in the other. One by one he threw the toys into the water for Marie to retrieve. He looked coy and playful.

Something about the scene troubled Blessington, although he could not, in his state, quite reason what it was. He watched Freycinet take a few steps back and paw the deck like an angry bull. In the next moment, Blessington realized what the problem was.

"Oh, Jesus Christ," he said.

Freycinet leaped into space. He still wore the greasy shorts he had worn the whole trip. In midair he locked his arms around his bent knees. He was holding a plastic spatula in his right hand. He hit the surface like a cannonball, raising a little waterspout, close enough to Marie to make her yelp.

"You know what?" Gillian asked. She had spotted it. She was amazing.

"Yes, I do. The ladder's still up. We forgot to lower it."

"Shit," she said and giggled.

Blessington turned over to float on his back and tried to calm himself. Overhead the sky was utterly cloudless. Moving his eyes only a little, he could see the great green tower of Gros Piton, shining like Jacob's ladder itself, thrusting toward the empty blue. Incredibly far above, a plane drew out its jet trail, a barely visible needle stitching the tiniest flaw in the vast perfect seamless curtain of day. Miles and miles above, beyond imagining.

"How we gonna get aboard?" Gillian asked. He did not care for the way she was acting in the water now, struggling to stay afloat, moving her arms too much, wasting her breath.

"We'll have to go up the float line. Or maybe," he said, "we can stand on each other's shoulders."

"I'm not," she said, gasping, "gonna like that too well."

"Take it easy, Gillian. Lie on your back."

What bothered him most was her laughing, a high-pitched giggle with each breath.

"OK, let's do it," she said, spitting salt water. "Let's do it before he does."

"Slow and steady," Blessington said.

They slowly swam together, breaststroking toward the boat. A late afternoon breeze had come up as the temperature began to fall.

Freycinet and Marie had allowed themselves to drift farther and farther from the boat. Blessington urged Gillian along beside him until the big white hull was between them and the other swimmers.

Climbing was impossible. It was partly the nature of the French-made boat: an unusually high transom and the rounded glassy hull made it particularly difficult to board except from a dock or a dinghy. That was the contemporary, security-conscious style. And the rental company had removed a few of the deck fittings that might have provided hand- and footholds. Still, he tried to find a grip so that Gillian could get on his shoulders. Once he even managed to position himself between her legs and push her a foot or so up the hull, as she sat on his shoulders. But there was nothing to grab on to and she was stoned. She swore and laughed and toppled off him.

He was swimming forward along the hull, looking for the float, when it occurred to him that the boat must be moving. Sure enough, holding his place, he could feel the hull sliding to windward under his hand. In a few strokes he was under the bow, feeling the ketch's weight thrusting forward, riding him down. Then he saw the Rastafarian float. It was unencumbered by any line. Honoré and Marie had not drifted from the boat — the boat itself was slowly blowing away, accompanied now by the screech of fiberglass against coral. The boys from the Pitons, having dealt with druggies before, had undone the mooring line while they were sleeping or nodding off or scarfing other sorts of lines.

Blessington hurried around the hull, with one hand to the boat's skin, trying to find the drifting float line. It might, he thought, be possible to struggle up along that. But there was no drifting float line. The boat boys must have uncleated it and balled the cleat in nylon line and silently tossed it aboard. He and Freycinet had been so feckless, the sea so glassy and the wind so low that the big boat had simply settled on the float, with its keel fast among the submerged elkhorn, and they had imagined themselves secured. The *Sans Regret,* to which he clung, was gone. Its teak interiors were in another world now, as far away as the tiny jet miles above them on its way to Brazil.

"It's no good," Blessington said to her.

"It's not?" She giggled.

"Please," he said, "please don't do that."

She gasped. "What?"

"Never mind," he said. "Come with me."

They had just started to swim away when a sudden breeze carried the *Sans Regret* from between the two couples, leaving Blessington and Gillian and Honoré and Marie to face one another in the water across a distance of twenty yards or so. Honoré and Marie stared at their shipmates in confusion. It was an embarrassing moment. Gillian laughed.

"What have you done?" Honoré asked Blessington. Blessington tried not to look at him.

"Come on," he said to Gillian. "Follow me."

Cursing in French, Freycinet started kicking furiously for the boat. Marie, looking very serious, struck out behind him. Gillian stopped to look after them.

Blessington glanced at his diver's watch. It was five-fifteen.

"Never mind them," he said. "Don't look at them. Stay with me."

He turned over on his back and commenced an artless backstroke, arms out straight, rowing with his palms, paddling with his feet. It was the most economic stroke he knew, the one he felt most comfortable with. He tried to make the strokes controlled and rhythmic rather than random and splashy to avoid conveying any impression of panic or desperation. To free his mind, he tried counting the strokes. As soon as they were over deep water, he felt the current. He tried to take it at a 45-degree angle, determining his bearing and progress by the great mountain overhead.

"Are you all right?" he asked Gillian. He raised his head to have a look at her. She was swimming in what looked like a good strong crawl. She coughed from time to time.

"I'm cold," she said. "That's the trouble."

"Try resting on your back," he said, "and paddling with your open hands. Like you were rowing."

She turned over and closed her eyes and smiled.

"I could go to sleep."

"You'll sleep ashore," he said. "Keep paddling."

They heard Freycinet cursing. Marie began to scream over and over again. It sounded fairly far away.

Checking on the mountain, Blessington felt a rush of despair. The lower slopes of the jungle were turning dark green. The line dividing sun-bright vegetation from deep-shaded green was withdrawing toward the peak. And the mountain looked no closer. He felt as though they were losing distance, being carried out faster than they could paddle. Marie's relentless screeches went on and on. Perhaps they were actually growing closer, Blessington thought, perhaps an evening tide was carrying them out.

"Poor kid," Gillian said. "Poor little baby."

"Don't listen," he said.

Gillian kept coughing, sputtering. He stopped asking her if she was all right.

"I'm sorry," she said. "I'm really cold now. I thought the water was warm at first."

"We're almost there," he said.

Gillian stopped swimming and looked up at Gros Piton. Turning over again to swim, she got a mouthful of water.

"Like . . . hell," she said.

"Keep going, Gillian."

It seemed to him, as he rowed the sodden vessel of his body and mind, that the sky was darkening. The sun's mark withdrew higher on the slopes. Marie kept screaming. They heard splashes far off where the boat was now. Marie and Honoré were clinging to it.

"Liam," Gillian said, "you can't save me."

"You'll save yourself," he said. "You'll just go on."

"I can't."

"Don't be a bloody stupid bitch."

"I don't think so," she said. "I really don't."

He stopped rowing himself then, although he was loath to. Every interruption of their forward motion put them more at the mercy of the current. According to the cruise book it was only a five-knot current but it felt much stronger. Probably reinforced by a tide.

Gillian was struggling, coughing in fits. She held her head up, greedy for air, her mouth open like a baby bird's in hope of nourishment. Blessington swam nearer her. The sense of their time ticking away, of distance lost to the current, enraged him.

"You've got to turn over on your back," he said gently. "Just ease onto your back and rest there. Then arch your back. Let your head lie backward so your forehead's in the water."

Trying to do as he told her, she began to thrash in a tangle of her own arms and legs. She swallowed water, gasped. Then she laughed again.

"Don't," he whispered.

"Liam? Can I rest on you?"

He stopped swimming toward her.

"You mustn't. You mustn't touch me. We mustn't touch each other. We might . . ."

"Please," she said.

"No. Get on your back. Turn over slowly."

Something broke the water near them. He thought it was the fin of a blacktip shark. A troublesome shark but not among the most dangerous. Of course, it could have been anything. Gillian still had the Rasta bracelet around her wrist.

"This is the thing, Liam. I think I got a cramp. I'm so dizzy."

"On your back, love. You must. It's the only way."

"No," she said. "I'm too cold. I'm too dizzy."

"Come on," he said. He started swimming again. Away from her.

"I'm so dizzy. I could go right out."

In mounting panic, he reversed direction and swam back toward her.

"Oh, shit," she said. "Liam?"

"I'm here."

"I'm fading out, Liam. I'll let it take me."

"Get on your back," he screamed at her. "You can easily swim. If you have to swim all night."

"Oh, shit," she said. Then she began to laugh again. She raised the hand that had the Rasta bracelet and splashed a sign of the cross.

"*Nam,*" she said. "*Nam myoho renge kyo.* Son of a bitch." Laughing. What she tried to say next was washed out of her mouth by a wave.

"I can just go out," she said. "I'm so dizzy."

Then she began to struggle and laugh and cry.

"Praise God, from whom all blessings flow," she sang, laughing. "Praise him, all creatures here below."

"Gillian," he said. "For God's sake." Maybe I can take her in, he thought. But that was madness and he kept his distance.

She was laughing and shouting at the top of her voice.

"Praise him above, you heavenly host! Praise Father, Son and Holy Ghost."

Laughing, thrashing, she went under, her face straining, wide-eyed. Blessington tried to look away but it was too late. He was afraid to go after her.

He lost his own balance then. His physical discipline collapsed and he began to wallow and thrash as she had.

"Help!" he yelled piteously. He was answered by a splash and Marie's screams. Perhaps now he only imagined them.

Eventually he got himself under control. When the entire mountain had subsided into dark green, he felt the pull of the current release him. The breakers were beginning to carry him closer to the sand, toward the last spit of sandy beach remaining on the island. The entire northern horizon was subsumed in the mountain overhead, Gros Piton.

He had one final mad moment. Fifty yards offshore, a riptide was running; it seized him and carried him behind the tip of the island. He had just enough strength and coherence of mind to swim across it. The sun was setting as he waded out, among sea grape and manchineel. When he turned he could see against the setting sun the bare poles of the *Sans Regret*, settled on the larger reef to the south of the island. It seemed to him also that he could make out a struggling human figure, dark against the light hull. But the dark came down quickly. He thought he detected a flash of green. Sometimes he thought he could still hear Marie screaming.

All night, as he rattled through the thick brush looking for a road to follow from concealment, Gillian's last hymn echoed in his mind's ear. He could see her dying face against the black fields of sugarcane through which he trudged.

Once he heard what he was certain was the trumpeting of an elephant. It made him believe, in his growing delirium, that he was in Africa — Africa, where he had never been. He hummed the hymn. Then he remembered he had read somewhere that the resort maintained an elephant in the bush. But he did not want to meet it, so he decided to stay where he was and wait for morning. All night he talked to Gillian, joked and sang hymns with her. He saved her again and again and they were together.

In the morning, when the sun rose fresh and full of promise, he set out for the Irish bar in Soufrière. He thought that they might overstand him there.

AQUARIUS OBSCURED

IN THE HOUSE on Noe Street, Big Gene was crooning into the telephone.

"Geerat, Geeroot. Neexat, Nixoot."

He hung up and patted a tattoo atop the receiver, sounding the cymbal beat by forcing air through his molars.

"That's how the Dutch people talk," he told Alison. "Keroot. Badoot. Krackeroot."

"Who was it?"

He lay back on the corduroy cushions and vigorously scratched himself. A smile spread across his face and he wiggled with pleasure, his eyelids fluttering.

"Some no-nut fool. Easy tool. Uncool."

He lay still with his mouth open, waiting for rhyming characterizations to emerge.

"Was it for me?"

When he looked at her, his eyes were filled with tears. He shook his head sadly to indicate that her questions were obviated by his sublime indifference.

Alison cursed him.

"Don't answer the fucking phone if you don't want to talk," she said. "It might be something important."

Big Gene remained supine.

"I don't know where you get off," he said absently. "See you reverting to typical boojwa. Reverting to type. Lost your fire."

His junkie mumble infuriated Alison. She snorted with exasperation.

"For Christ's sake!"

"You bring me down so bad," Gene said softly. "I don't need you. I got control, you know what I mean?"

"It's ridiculous," she told him. "Talking to you is a complete waste of time."

As she went into the next room she heard him moan, a lugubrious, falsetto coo incongruent with his bulk but utterly expressive of the man he had become. His needles had punctured him.

In the bedroom, Io was awake; her large brown eyes gazed fearfully through crib bars at the sunlit window.

"Hello, sweetie," Alison said.

Io turned solemnly toward her mother and yawned.

A person here, Alison thought, lifting her over the bars, the bean blossomed. Walks and conversation. The end of our Madonna-and-child number. A feather of panic fluttered in her throat.

"Io," she told her daughter, "we have got to get our shit together here."

The scene was crumbling. Strong men had folded like stage flats, legality and common sense were fled. Cerebration flickered.

Why me, she demanded of herself, walking Io to the potty. Why do I have to be the only one with any smarts?

On the potty, Io delivered. Alison wiped her and flushed the toilet. By training Alison was an astronomer, but she had never practiced.

Io could dress herself except for the shoes. When Alison tied them, it was apparent to her that they would shortly be too small.

"What'll we do?" she asked Io with a playful but genuinely frightened whine.

"See the fishies," Io said.

"See the fishies?" Alison stroked her chin, burlesquing a thoughtful demeanor, rubbing noses with Io to make her smile. "Good Lord."

Io drew back and nodded soberly.

"See the fishies."

At that moment, Alison recalled the fragment of an undersea dream. Something in the dream had been particularly agreeable and its recall afforded her a happy little throb.

"Well that's what we'll do," she told Io. "We'll go to the aquarium. A capital idea."

"Yes," Io said.

Just outside Io's room, on the littered remnant of a sundeck, lived a vicious and unhygienic Doberman, who had been named Buck after a dog Big Gene claimed to have once owned in Aruba. Alison opened the sliding glass door to admit it, and watched nervously as it nuzzled Io.

"Buck," Io said without enthusiasm.

Alison seized the dog by its collar and thrust it out the bedroom door before her.

In the living room, Big Gene was rising from the cushions, a cetaceous surfacing.

"Buck, my main man," he sang. "Bucky bonaroo."

"How about staying with him today?" Alison said. "I want to take Io to the aquarium."

"Not I," Gene declared. "Noo."

"Why the hell not?" Alison asked savagely.

"Cannot be."

"Shit! I can't leave him alone here, he'll wreck the place. How can I take him to the goddamn aquarium?"

Gene shrugged sleepily.

"Ain't this the night you get paid?" he asked after a moment.

"Yeah," Alison said.

In fact, Alison had been paid the night before, her employer having thrown some eighty dollars' worth of half-dollars full into her face. There had been a difference of opinion regarding Alison's performance as a danseuse, and she had spoken sharply with Mert the Manager. Mert had replied in an incredibly brutal and hostile manner, had fired her, insulted her breasts and left her to peel coins from the soiled floor until the profile of Jack Kennedy was welded to her mind's eye. She had not mentioned the incident to Gene; the half-dollars were concealed under the rubber sheet beneath Io's mattress.

"Good," Gene said. "Because I got to see the man then."

He was looking down at Io, and Alison watched him for signs of resentment or contempt but she saw only sadness, sickness in his face. Io paid him no attention at all.

It was startling the way he had mellowed out behind smack. Witnessing it, she had almost forgiven him the punches, and she had noticed for the first time that he had rather a kind heart. But he stole and was feckless; his presence embarrassed her.

"How'm I going to take a dog to the aquarium, for Christ's sake?"

The prospect of having Buck along irritated Alison sorely. In her irritation, she decided that the thing might be more gracefully endured with the white-cross jobbers. The white-cross jobbers were synthetics manufactured by a mad chemist in Hayward. Big Gene called them IT-390 to distinguish them from IT-290, which they had turned out, upon consumption, not to be.

She took a handful from the saki jar in which they were stored and downed them with tap water.

"All right, *Buck*," she called, pronouncing the animal's name with distaste, "goddamn it." She put his leash on, sent Io ahead to the car and pulled the reluctant dog out behind her.

With Io strapped in the passenger seat and Buck cringing under the dashboard, Alison ran Lombard Street in the outside lane, accelerating on the curves like a racing driver. She drove hard to stay ahead of the drug's rush. When she pulled up in the aquarium's parking lot, her mouth had gone dry and the little Sanctus bells of adjusted alertness had begun to tinkle. She hurried them under wind-rattled eucalyptus and up the massive steps that led to the building's Corinthian portico.

"Now where are we going to put this goddamn dog?" she asked Io. When she blinked, her eyeballs clicked. I've done it, she thought. I've swallowed it again. Vandalism.

After a moment's confused hesitation, she led Buck to one side of the entrance and secured his chain round a brass hydrant fixture with a carefully worked running clove hitch. The task brought to her recollection a freakish afternoon when she had tied Buck in front of a bar on El Camino. For the protection of passersby, she had fashioned a sign from the cardboard backing of a foolscap tablet and written on it with a green felt-tipped pen — DO NOT TRY TO PET THIS DOG. Her last memory of the day was watching the sign blow away across the street and past the pumps of an Exxon station.

Buck's vindictive howls pursued them to the oxidized-copper doors of the main entrance.

It was early morning and the aquarium was uncrowded. Liquefactious sounds ran up and down the smooth walls, child voices ricocheted from the ceiling. Holding Io by the hand, Alison wandered through the interior twilight, past tanks of sea horses, scorpion fish, African tilapia. Pausing before an endlessly gyrating school of salmon, she saw that some of the fish were eyeless, the sockets empty and perfectly cleaned. The blind fish swam with the rest, staying in line, turning with the school.

Io appeared not to notice them.

In the next hall, Alison halted her daughter before each tank, reading from the lighted presentation the name of the animal contained, its habitat and Latin name. The child regarded all with gravity.

At the end of the east wing was a room brighter than the rest; it was the room in which porpoises lived in tanks that were open to the sky. As Alison entered it, she experienced a curiously pleasant sensation.

"Look," she said to Io. "Dolphins."

"Dolphins?"

They walked up to the glass of the largest tank; its lower area was fouled with small handprints. Within, a solitary blue-gray beast was rounding furiously, describing gorgeous curves with figure eights, skimming the walls at half an inch's distance. Alison's mouth opened in awe.

"An Atlantic Dolphin," she told Io in a soft, reverential voice. "From the Atlantic Ocean. On the other side of America. Where Providence is."

"And Grandpa," Io said.

"And Grandpa is in Providence too."

For the space of several seconds, the dream feeling returned to her with an intensity that took her breath away. There had been some loving presence in it and a discovery.

She stared into the tank until the light that filtered through the churning water began to suggest the numinous. Io, perceiving that her mother was not about to move on, retraced her steps toward the halls through which they had come, and commenced seeing the fish over again. Whenever an aquarium-goer smiled at her, she looked away in terror.

Alison stood transfixed, trying to force recall. It had been something special, something important. But silly — as with dreams. She found herself laughing and then, in the next moment, numb with loss as the dream's sense faded. Her heart was racing with the drug.

God, she thought, it's all just flashes and fits. We're just out here in this shit.

With sudden horror, she realized at once that there had been another part of the dream and that it involved the fact that she and Io were just out there and that this was not a dream from which one awakened. Because one *was*, after all.

She turned anxiously to look for Io and saw the child several galleries back, standing in front of the tank where the blind fish were.

The dream had been about getting out of it, trying to come in and make it stop. In the end, when it was most terrible, she had been mercifully carried into a presence before which things had been resolved. The memory of that resolution made her want to weep.

Her eye fell on the animal in the tank. She followed its flights and charges with fascination.

There had been some sort of communication, with or without words.

A trained scientist, Alison loved logic above all else; it was her only important pleasure. If the part about one being out there was true — and it was — what then about the resolution? It seemed to her, as she watched the porpoise, that even dreamed things must have their origin in a kind of truth, that no level of the mind was capable of utterly unfounded construction. Even hallucinations — phenomena with which Alison had become drearily familiar — needed their origins in the empirically verifiable — a cast of light, a sound on the wind. Somehow, she thought, somewhere in the universe, the resolving presence must exist.

Her thoughts raced, and she licked her lips to cool the sere dryness cracking them. Her heart gave a desperate leap.

"Was it you?" she asked the porpoise.

"Yes," she heard him say. "Yes, it was."

Alison burst into tears. When she had finished sobbing, she took a Kleenex from her bag, wiped her eyes and leaned against the cool marble beside the tank.

Prepsychosis. Disorders of thought. Failure to abstract.

"This is ridiculous," she said.

From deep within, from the dreaming place, sounded a voice.

"You're here," the porpoise told her. "That's what matters now."

Nothing in the creature's manner suggested communication or even the faintest sentience. But human attitudes of engagement, Alison reminded herself, were not to be expected. To expect them was anthropocentrism — a limiting, reactionary position like ethnocentrism or sexism.

"It's very hard for me," she told the porpoise. "I can't communicate well at the best of times. And an aquarium situation is pretty weird." At a loss for further words, Alison fell back on indignation. "It must be awful for you."

"It's somewhat weird," she understood the porpoise to say. "I wouldn't call it awful."

Alison trembled.

"But . . . how can it not be awful? A conscious mind shut up in a tank with stupid people staring at you? Not," she hastened to add, "that I think I'm any better. But the way you're stuck in here with these slimy, repulsive fish."

"I don't find fish slimy and repulsive," the porpoise told her.

Mortified, Alison began to stammer an apology, but the creature cut her off. "The only fish I see are the ones they feed me. It's people I see all day. I wonder if you can realize how *dry* you all are."

"Good Lord!" She moved closer to the tank. "You must hate us."

She became aware of laughter.

"I don't hate."

Alison's pleasure at receiving this information was tempered by a political anxiety. The beast's complacency suggested something objectionable; the suspicion clouded her mind that her interlocutor might be a mere Aquarium Porpoise, a deracinated stooge, an Uncle —

The laughter sounded again.

"I'm sorry," Alison said. "My head is full of such shit."

"Our condition is profoundly different from yours. We don't require the same things. Our souls are as different from yours as our bodies are."

"I have the feeling," Alison said, "that yours are better."

"I think they are. But I'm a porpoise."

The animal in the tank darted upward, torpedolike, toward the fog-colored surface, then plunged again in a column of spinning, bubbling foam.

"You called me here, didn't you?" Alison asked. "You wanted me to come."

"In a way."

"Only in a way?"

"We communicated our presence here. A number of you might have responded. Personally, I'm satisfied that it was yourself."

"Are you?" Alison cried joyfully. She was aware that her words echoed through the great room. "You see, I asked because I've been having these dreams. Odd things have been happening to me." She paused thoughtfully. "Like I've been listening to the radio sometimes and I've heard these wild things — like just for a second. As though there's been kind of a pattern. Was it you guys?"

"Some of the time. We have our ways."

"Then," she asked breathlessly, "why me?"

"Don't you know why?" the beast asked softly.

"It must have been because you knew I would understand."

There was no response.

"It must have been because you knew how much I hate the way things are with us. Because you knew I'd listen. Because I need something so much."

"Yet," the porpoise said sternly, "you made things this way. You thought you needed them the way they are."

"It wasn't me," Alison said. "Not me. I don't need this shit."

Wide-eyed, she watched him shoot for the surface again, then dive and skim over the floor of his tank, rounding smartly at the wall.

"I love you," she declared suddenly. "I mean, I feel a great love for you and I feel there is a great lovingness in you. I just know that there's something really super-important that I can learn from you."

"Are you prepared to know how it is with us?"

"Yes," Alison said. "Oh, yes. And what I can do."

"You can be free," the animal said. "You can learn to perceive in a new way."

Alison became aware of Io standing beside her, frowning up at her tears. She bent down and put her head next to the child's.

"Io, can you see the dolphin? Do you like him?"

"Yes," Io said.

Alison stood up.

"My daughter," she told her dolphin.

Io watched the animal contentedly for a while and then went to sit on a bench in the back of the hall.

"She's only three and a half," Alison said. She feared that communion might be suspended on the introduction of a third party. "Do you like her?"

"We see a great many of your children," the beast replied. "I can't answer you in those terms."

Alison became anxious.

"Does that mean that you don't have *any* emotions? That you can't love?"

"Were I to answer yes or no I would deceive you either way. Let's say only that we don't make the same distinctions."

"I don't understand," Alison said. "I suppose I'm not ready to."

"As your perception changes," the porpoise told her, "many things will seem strange and unfamiliar. You must unlearn old structures of thought that have been forced on you. Much faith, much resolution will be required."

"I'll resist," Alison admitted sadly. "I know I will. I'm very skeptical and frivolous by nature. And it's all so strange and wonderful that I can't believe it."

"All doubt is the product of your animal nature. You must rise above your species. You must trust those who instruct you."

"I'll try," Alison said resolutely. "But it's so incredible! I mean, for all these centuries you guys and us have been the only aware species on the planet, and now we've finally come together! It just blows my mind that here — now — for the first time . . ."

"What makes you think it's the first time?"

"Good Lord!" Alison exclaimed. "It's not the first time?"

"There were others before you, Alison. They were weak and fickle. We lost them."

Alison's heart chilled at his words.

"But hasn't it ever worked?"

"It's in the nature of your species to conceive enthusiasms and then to weary of them. Your souls are self-indulgent and your concentration feeble. None of you has ever stayed with it."

"I will," Alison cried. "I'm unique and irreplaceable, and nothing could be more important than this. Understanding, responding inside — that's my great talent. I can do it!"

"We believe you, Alison. That's why you're here."

She was flooded with her dreaming joy. She turned quickly to

look for Io and saw her lying at full length on the bench, staring
up into the overhead lights. Near her stood a tall, long-haired
young man who was watching Alison. His stare was a profane
irritation and Alison forced it from her mind, but her mood
turned suddenly militant.

"I know it's not important in your terms," she told the porpoise, "but it infuriates me to see you shut up like this. You must
miss the open sea so much."

"I've never left it," the animal said, "and your pity is wasted
on me. I am here on the business of my race."

"I guess it's the way I was brought up. I had a lousy upbringing, but some things about it were good. See, my father, he's a
real asshole but he's what we call a liberal. He taught me to
really hate it when somebody was oppressed. Injustice makes
me want to fight. I suppose it sounds stupid and trivial to you,
but that's how it is with me."

The dolphin's voice was low and soothing, infinitely kind.
"We know how it is with you. You understand nothing of your
own behavior. Everything you think and do merely reflects what
is known to us as a Dry Posture. Your inner life, your entire
history are nothing more than that."

"Good Lord!" Alison said. "Dry Posture."

"As we work with you, you must bear this in mind. You must
discover the quality of Dry Posture in all your thoughts and
actions. When you have separated this quality from your soul,
what remains will be the bond between us. At that point your
life will truly begin."

"Dry Posture," Alison said. "Wow!"

The animal in the tank was disporting itself just below the
surface. In her mounting enthusiasm Alison became increasingly frustrated by the fact that its blank, good-humored face
appeared totally oblivious of her presence. She reminded herself
again that the hollow dissembling of human facial expression

was beneath its nature, and welcomed the opportunity to be divested of a Dry Posture.

The silence from which the dolphin spoke became charged with music.

"In the sea lies our common origin," she heard him say. "In the sea all was once One. In the sea find your surrender — in surrender find victory, renewal, survival. Recall the sea! Recall our common heartbeat! Return to the peace of primordial consciousness!"

"Oh, how beautiful," Alison cried, her own consciousness awash in salt flumes of insight.

"Our lousy Western culture is worthless," she declared fervently. "It's rotten and sick. We've got to get back. Please," she implored the dolphin, "tell us how!"

"If you receive the knowledge," the animal told her, "your life will become one of dedication and struggle. Are you ready to undertake such striving?"

"Yes," Alison said. "Yes!"

"Are you willing to serve that force which relentlessly wills the progress of the conscious universe?"

"With all my heart!"

"Willing to surrender to that sublime destiny which your species has so fecklessly denied?"

"Oh, boy," Alison said, "I surely am."

"Excellent," said the porpoise. "It shall be your privilege to assist the indomitable will of a mighty and superior species. The natural order shall be restored. That which is strong and sound shall dominate. That which is weak and decadent shall perish and disappear."

"Right on!" Alison cried. She felt her shoulders squaring, her heels coming together.

"Millennia of usurpation shall be overturned in a final solution!"

"Yeah," Alison said. "By any means necessary."

It seemed to Alison that she detected in the porpoise's speech a foreign accent — if not a Third World accent, at least the accent of a civilization older and more together than her own.

"So," the porpoise continued, "where your cities and banks, your aquaria and museums now stand, there shall be rubble only. The responsibility shall rest exclusively with humankind, for our patience has been thoroughly exhausted. What we have not achieved through striving for equitable dialogue, we shall now achieve by striving of another sort."

Alison listened in astonishment as the music's volume swelled behind her eyes.

"For it is our belief," the porpoise informed her, "that in strife, life finds its purification." His distant, euphonious voice assumed a shrill, hysterical note. "In the discipline of ruthless struggle, history is forged and the will tempered! Let the craven, the once-born, shirk the fray — we ourselves shall strike without mercy at the sniveling mass of our natural inferiors. Triumph is our destiny!"

Alison shook her head in confusion.

"Whoa," she said.

Closing her eyes for a moment, she beheld with startling clarity the image of a blond-bearded man wearing a white turtleneck sweater and a peaked officer's cap. His face was distended with fury; beside him loomed a gray cylindrical form that might have been a periscope. Alison opened her eyes quickly and saw the porpoise blithely coursing the walls of its tank.

"But that's not love or life or anything," she sobbed. "That's just cruelty."

"Alison, baby, don't you know it's all the same? Without cruelty you can't have love. If you're not ready to destroy someone, then you're not ready to love them. Because if you've got the knowledge — you know, like if you really have it — then if you do what you have to do that's just everybody's karma. If you have to waste somebody because the universe wills it, then it's just like the bad part of yourself that you're wasting. It's an act of love."

In the next instant, she saw the bearded man again. His drawn, evil face was bathed in a sinister, submarine light, reflected from God knew what fiendish instruments of death.

"I know what you are," Alison called out in horror. "You're a fascist!"

When the beast spoke once more, the softness had vanished from its voice.

"Your civilization has afforded us many moments of amusement. Unfortunately, it must now be irrevocably destroyed."

"Fascist!" Alison whimpered in a strangled voice. "Nazi!"

"Peace," the porpoise intoned, and the music behind him turned tranquil and low. "Here is the knowledge. You must say it daily."

Enraged now, she could detect the mocking hypocrisy in his false, mellow tones:

> Surrender to the Notion
> Of the Motion of the Ocean.

As soon as she received the words, they occupied every fraction of her inner space, reverberating moronically, over and over. She put her hands over her ears.

"Horseshit!" she cried. "What kind of cheapo routine is that?"

The voice, she suspected suddenly, might not be that of a porpoise. It might be the man in the turtleneck.

But where? Hovering at the mouth of a celestial black hole, secure within the adjoining dimension? A few miles off Sausalito at periscope depth? Or — more monstrous — ingeniously reduced in size and concealed within the dolphin?

"Help," Alison called softly.

At the risk of permanent damage, she desperately engaged her linear perception. Someone might have to know.

"I'm caught up in this plot," she reported. "Either porpoises are trying to reach me with this fascist message or there's some kind of super-Nazi submarine offshore."

Exhausted, she rummaged through her knit bag for a cigarette, found one and lit it. A momentary warp, she assured herself, inhaling deeply. A trifling skull pop, perhaps an air bubble. She smoked and trembled, avoiding the sight of the tank.

In the next moment, she became aware that the tall young man she had seen earlier had made a circuit of the hall and was standing beside her.

"Fish are groovy," the young man said.

"Wait a minute," Alison demanded. "Just wait a minute here. Was that . . . ?"

The young man displayed a woodchuck smile.

"You were really tripping on those fish, right? Are you stoned?"

He carried a camera case on a strap round his shoulder and a black cape slung over one arm.

"I don't know what you're talking about," Alison said. She was suddenly consumed with loathing.

"No? 'Cause you look really spaced out."

"Well, I'm not," Alison said firmly. She saw Io advancing from the bench.

The young man stood by as Io clutched her mother's floor-length skirt.

"I want to go outside now," Io said.

His pink smile expanded and he descended quickly to his haunches to address Io at her own level.

"Hiya, baby. My name's Andy."

Io had a look at Andy and attempted flight. Alison was holding one of her hands; Andy made her fast by the other.

"I been taking pictures," he told her. "Pictures of the fishies."

He pursued Io to a point behind Alison's knees. Alison pulled on Io's free hand and found herself staring down into the camera case.

"You like the fishies?" Andy insisted. "You think they're groovy?"

There were two Nikon lenses side by side in the case. Alison let Io's hand go, thrust her own into the case and plucked out a lens. While Andy was asking Io if she was shy, Alison dropped the lens into her knit bag. As Andy started up, she seized the second lens and pressed it hard against her skirt.

Back on his feet, Andy was slightly breathless.

"You wanna go smoke some dope?" he asked Alison. "I'm goin' over to the art museum and sneak some shots over there. You wanna come?"

"Actually," Alison told him, "I have a luncheon engagement."

Andy blinked. "Far out."

"Far out?" Alison asked. "I'll tell you something far out, Andy. There is a lot of really repulsive shit in this aquarium, Andy. There are some very low-level animals here and they're very frightening and unreal. But there isn't one thing in this place that is as repulsive and unreal as you are, Andy."

She heard the laughter echo and realized that it was her own. She clenched her teeth to stop it.

"You should have a tank of your own, Andy."

As she led Io toward the door, she cupped the hand that held the second lens against her hip, like a mannequin. At the end of the hall, she glanced back and saw Andy looking into the dolphin's tank. The smile on his face was dreadful.

"I like the fish," Io said as they descended the pompous stone steps outside the entrance. "I like the lights in the fish places."

Recognizing them, Buck rushed forward on his chain, his tongue dripping. Alison untied him as quickly and calmly as she could.

"We'll come back, sweetie," she said. "We'll come back lots of times."

"Tomorrow?" the child asked.

In the parking lot, Alison looked over her shoulder. The steps were empty; there were no alarums or pursuits.

When they were in the car, she felt cold. Columns of fog were moving in from the bay. She sat motionless for a while, blew her nose and wrapped a spare sweater that was lying on the seat around Io's shoulders.

"Mama's deluded," she explained.

BEAR AND
HIS DAUGHTER

‒‒‒‒‒‒‒‒‒

➤

I T WAS AN old Mafia lodge on the north shore of the lake that went back to the 1940s. During the years of its construction casino managements had not yet discovered the necessity of isolating their patrons from time and daylight, so the main bar had a huge picture window fronting on the lambent water and the towering sierra beyond it. The sun had already disappeared behind the mountains and the lake was purple with dusk. Smart, the bearded poet, stood with a double Scotch and water in his hand, his stool turned to the window.

"Wine-dark!" he exclaimed to the bartender.

The bartender, a foxy-faced young man, had a short, military-style haircut but his manner was slack in the extreme.

"Say again, señor?"

"Wine-dark," Smart repeated, gesturing toward the lake.

The young bartender seemed virtually floored by the assault of sudden illumination.

"Wine-dark? The lake? You see it as like 'wine-dark'?"

"Not really an original conceit," Smart explained. "Actually..."

"Wine-fucking-dark." He gave a little half-dazzled toss of his narrow head. "Whoa." They had been alone at the bar but shortly a cocktail waitress with reddish-blond bangs arrived to collect an order.

"Señor here," the bartender told her, "sees the lake as 'wine-dark.'"

"Cool," the young woman said. She looked at Smart not unkindly.

"Make you feel like another belt, señor?" asked the barkeep.

"Sure," said Smart.

The barman poured Smart the mean measure prescribed by the house. Smart reminded him to make it a double.

"Then it'll be Scotch-dark, right?" the youth asked.

"And then it'll be just dark," said the waitress. She put her order on a tray and sailed off to deliver it.

A few minutes into his third double Scotch, Smart asked the young man, "Think there are any salmon left in the lake?"

At first the bartender seemed unclear as to what such creatures might be. Then he said, "Hey, sure. All you want." He studied Smart for a moment. "Salmon? That what you like?"

"Yes," Smart said. "Salmon are what I like. Salmon are what I go for."

"No shit?" asked the man.

For the past year, Smart had been trying to reconstruct a poem he had written about witnessing the salmon migration in the Tanana River in central Alaska thirty years before. It had been two-thirty or three on an early summer morning. The sun had been low on the horizon, and on the distant tundra a herd of bison were grazing the bitter subarctic bush. The fish working their way upstream had been plainly visible through the clear water. They were survivors, veterans of the Pacific, two hundred miles from the sea now, returned to die in the place they were spawned. Above them gulls, eagles, ospreys wheeled in numbers such as Smart had never encountered. It seemed to him that he had never witnessed a sight so moving and noble as

the last progress of these salmon. So he had written a poem and
left it somewhere and never seen it again:

> Like elephants, swaying
> Straining with the effort of each undulation,
> They labor home . . .

"Check the dining room," the bartender said. "You never can
tell. Me, I don't go for fish." He lowered his voice. "If I did,
man, I wouldn't have it here. But the steak, hey, that's another
story. The steak is straight from Kansas City, you know what
I'm saying?"

"The river is forever swift and young," Smart remembered he
had written, "forever renewed, beyond history."

He looked out into the darkness, as though he might find the
rest of the words there.

> But these, elephant-eyed
> Under the skirl and whirl and screech of gulls
> And swoop of eagles,
> Are creatures of time's wheel.

"I bet they got trout," the bartender said. "They always do.
But I can't like give you trout out here. You gotta go to the
dining room. You see where the maitre d' is standing?"

Smart, disoriented for a moment, looked toward a man in a
dinner jacket far across the room. Now it all had to be paid for,
he thought, every worthwhile moment, every line, good, bad,
mediocre. And of all the poems, why had he to lose that one?

"Under the pale ultra-planetary sky of the white night," it
had gone on, more or less:

> I feel for them such love
> And, for their cold struggle, such admiration
> In my overheated heart.

Smart rose from his stool, dizzy with the Scotch and the altitude.

"You OK, señor?" asked the bartender.

He fixed the youth with a glittering eye, tossed a few singles on the bar and strolled out to the casino. On the way, he passed the young cocktail waitress.

"You got nice eyes," she told him.

He felt so pleased he could only smile. A man had to keep settling for less. Patronizing compliments. You became a few scattered lines of your own poem.

> What wisdom could be bound in a fish eye?
> It must be an illusion.
> For how could fish, these fish, under their long-lost
>   ale-colored sky,
> In the strange light, coming home, coming back after
>   all these years,
> Have something in their cold old eyes I need
> Or think I need?

A magical experience it had been, that night, all poetry and light!

The casino had an Old West theme, with wagon-wheel chandeliers and fake Navajo rugs and buffalo skulls and elkhorn racks fixed to the log walls. It was a quiet weekday night on the lake and the action was slow. Half a dozen blackjack games were under way, dealt by fair young women with cavalier curls and sleeve garters. Three roulette wheels stood motionless beneath transparent plastic covers. At the craps table, two silent men, a pit boss and a stick man, stood side by side like mourners. Smart, who had carried his drink from the bar, leaned against a polished pine stanchion to watch them.

The house uniform was country-and-western. The pit boss was a pale, yellowing man in a two-tone beige and tan jacket and a bolo tie with a turquoise ornament. The stick man wore a red bandanna knotted below his Adam's apple. He was bald and red-faced. There were shiny scars on the taut skin over his cheekbones. Smart decided to play.

He was midway through a six-college tour of the mountain states, his first reading series in three years. For each reading, Smart was being paid two thousand dollars. He hitched up his chino trousers and advanced to the table.

"Right," he declared. "A wager here."

The men turned serpent gazes on him.

"Did you want to play, friend?" the stick man asked.

"Please," said Smart. "Five-dollar chips."

"Friend will play," sang the stick man in a grifter's croon. He pushed the big red dice toward Smart. Smart spread ten chips along the Pass line, took up the dice, shook them and rolled.

"Come-out roll," the stick man intoned. The voice conveyed to Smart the romance of his own youth — carnivals, the society of car thieves and hustlers, the street.

"A seven-ah," the man declared, for Smart had rolled four and tray. He pushed Smart's winnings along the green baize. Smart rolled again. The dice read double fives.

"Ten the point," declared the stick man. "Ten the hard way."

On the very next roll Smart threw another ten. The stick man paid out his chips. Smart left his winnings in place and rolled eleven.

"An ee-leven," the stick man called. Smart gave the man a humorous glance, as though his good fortune were somehow being appreciated. The man's dead eyes offered neither help nor hope and not a grain of congratulation.

A pretty girl in a leotard, a different girl this time and not the one who admired his eyes, asked Smart if he would like a drink. She was olive-skinned but pale, with an unhappy smile. Drugs, he suspected.

"Oh," said the poet, "double Scotch, I think."

And about halfway through the next anemic double Scotch,

a drink for which Smart could conceive scant respect, things started to go wrong. Looking at the table, he found he could not calculate the amount of money represented by the chips there. The stick man had changed some of his five-dollar chips to twenty-fives, yellow chips with metal centers. Uncertainly he drew back some of the chips and let some ride. He rolled boxcars, then a seven, and lost.

For a moment he hesitated. Sensing the house men's impatience, entirely to please them, he spread the rest of his cash along the Pass line. Then he rolled and won again. Adrenaline made his heart swell but the exhilaration cast a queer shadow. Other players arrived, nasal tourists, men in baseball caps, owlish women, betting against him. He became more and more confused. There was some kind of quarrel. The pit boss called for Security. There was such violence, such hatred in the boss's voice that Smart was briefly terrified. A woman laughed.

Suddenly he was being lifted off his feet. An enormous Chicano security guard in a tan uniform had gripped his arm. Smart was a large man but the guard was larger.

"Just a second," Smart said. "Just a minute." He had no choice but to move in the direction the guard impelled him. Otherwise, Smart felt, he would fall and be at the mercy of the whirling angry room. Looking up at the man holding him, Smart could focus on his face. It was brown and handsome, without expression.

"That's hard on the arm," he said, trying to laugh it off, sputtering too wetly. And then he saw that there was a second guard, a young woman with straight blond hair who was saying, "Are you not all right, sir? Because if you're not all right, sir, we'll have to put you in custody of the police and they can see you get whatever attention you might require, if you feel you require attention. That would just be a matter of your own protection, if you required custody. Do you think you require custody, sir? For your own protection?"

"All right," Smart said.

Then they were on the steps of the casino, at the edge of the parking lot beside the highway. The big Mexican stood by while the blond woman guard recited.

"Now sir, the hotel and lounge and casino and the restaurant and the grounds are private property and you may not enter them without permission and you do not have that permission now. And you are barred from those places at any time. And you are very close — this close, sir — to violating our laws and you will go to jail if we have to engage you personally again. So are you hearing me, sir?"

As Smart made his way toward his car, he turned and saw her, half in the shadow of her giant companion, talking into a hand radio.

"My daughter," he told the two guards, "is a park ranger. I'm on my way to see her."

The big Mexican guard advanced on him.

"How's that? How's that, buddy? You got a problem?"

"No, no," Smart implored. "No problem whatsoever."

He breathed with difficulty. A few years before he had suffered a breakdown and been involved in an accident. Now his arm was completely numb where the guard had grabbed it. Its throbbing kept time with the beating in his chest.

He climbed into his car and waited for the pair of them to go back inside. The worst of it, he thought, was their rage at him. As though everyone had been waiting for him to make the slightest wrong move. He started his engine, shifted into gear and, without turning on his headlights, guided the car to the part of the parking lot that was farthest from the highway. Beside the lot, beyond a log fence, began the stand of fir trees that marked the edge of woods that bordered the lake. Turning off the ignition was the last thing he remembered.

He dreamed of being in trouble — trouble in boot camp, trouble at sea, trouble among the stacked books on college library shelves. He was forever doing things wrong. Wronging students, brother poets, women. The world was rotten with anger.

Once he half awakened to a kind of clarity. He was still trying to remember the poem about salmon. Never published. Lost.

> And what they've seen!
> The shimmer of the equatorial moon against still glass
>   overhead
> And leapt, breathless, headlong, a hair ahead of the
>   needle jaws
> Out into the breathing world under the blank blessing of
>   the Southern Cross
> Out under Cygnus, Hydra, Hercules,
> Now close-hauled home.

It was red dawn when he came properly awake. He opened the car door and climbed out stiffly, shivering in the morning's cold. He had to pop the trunk and pull out his old seabag from among the empty suitcases he kept there and rummage through it for a sweater warm enough. As he was pulling the sweater over his head, a few details of the previous night came back to him. He sat sideways in the driver's seat with the car door open, feet on the ground, head in his hands. Then he looked up warily, wondering if he was still being stalked. But all that had happened concerned him less than the words of his lost poem.

It seemed a shame, he thought, to be denied the lake. He could feel its huge cold blue presence across the dark green zone beside the parking lot. There was no one in sight. Thirsty and sore, Smart climbed over the log fence into the gloom of the big trees. He found a trail at once and followed it. Only a few yards off the hotel lot the sense of deep forest closed around him. And the trail was so unlittered, it might have been backcountry. The hotel was not the sort whose guests took walks in the woods.

The trail led him to a granite ledge over the lake. In spite of the neatness of the trail, the lakeside was an untidy place, with spent Coors cans and pull-rings and a few crushed empty cigarette packs. Smart saw that a paved road led to the lake from the casino's drive. Above the mists over the still water, an osprey circled like some omen in a shaman's dream. The sun over the Washoes lit the white feathers beneath its wings.

He stood and watched the bird soar for a moment, then closed his eyes and breathed deeply.

Then he began to scramble down the granite ledge that led to the water. The lake was so still that there were barely wavelets against the rocky shore. In his morning thirst, Smart lay belly-down on the cold jagged stone and stretched out to drink. Pine needles floated in the shallows around him. He supposed it was inadvisable to drink the lake water but he was not in a mood to worry. It tasted sweet in his dry throat. Were there still landlocked salmon? There had been when he was a boy.

> Their hulking gray bodies
> Crisscrossed and creased with scars
> Of hook and teeth, harpoon, gaff and winch and bullet —
> They've survived the wolf shark's circling, the bitch seal's
>   guile to feed her pups,
> From the prison-yard frenzy in the ascending stifle of the net
> These broke free.

Getting to his feet, he wiped his mouth with his woolen sleeve and looked about him like an outlaw. Anyone spotting him there, burly and furtive in the early morning light, might have been reminded of a bear prowling at the edge of human habitation. In a stiff-legged lope, favoring his sore back, he hurried to his car. For a while he sat in indecision, hands on the wheel, breathing hard. Looking at his watch, he saw that it was after six. No longer too early to call his daughter, who lived within the State Natural Monument area, five hundred miles to the east and north. He drove for several miles along the road that circled the lake until he found a strip mall with a pay phone. From it, he called his daughter Rowan, named for the rowan tree. In the very first ring of her phone he could sense the desolation and terrible magic of the place she lived, the trailer under the stars, the fields of lava.

"Hi," said a man's voice when Rowan's line was answered. The casual response had a drawling near-insolence, somewhat mitigated by the softness of the speaker's voice. Smart recognized his daughter's friend and fellow ranger John Hears the Sun Come Up. John was a Shoshone from the reservation adjoining the monument who had gone east to college, at Beloit, and come home to work for the Park Service.

"John? Will Smart. What's new, brother?"

"A little here, a little there," said John Hears the Sun Come Up. "We been expecting you, sort of."

"Sort of?"

"I was surprised you were coming. Rowan, she says she always knew. Anyway, we got your phone message."

"Is it all right?"

There was a hesitation, and Smart was surprised and a little offended by it.

"Sure. She's real excited. Yeah," John said in his unhurried manner. "Real excited. I hope you have got some poems to read us."

"I would never come empty-handed," Smart said. "Tonight all right? I should be able to cover five hundred miles."

"Out here you should be able to cover a thousand. Just be careful."

"Oh, I will be," Smart said. "I'm sober again."

By lying, he had sought to reassure John. But he had also been trying to find out if Rowan, who shared his difficulty with alcohol and drugs, was on or off the wagon.

John seemed to understand.

"That's real good," he said. "Rowan's been sober a lot. But now she got a raw deal from the service. She got transferred to law enforcement and she's real pissed off."

"Law enforcement!" Smart exclaimed. "That's ridiculous."

"I know it," said John, "especially considering her. But, you know, they're short-handed. They're putting everybody in law enforcement. Biologists and historians. Men and women both. So she's pissed off. It's not for her."

"Right," Smart said. He supposed all this must mean she was drinking again. Possibly doing the crank brought over from the Pacific coast or made in the desert by bikers. "The public's getting out of line, I guess."

"Oh," John said, "the public's apeshit. So the state's bringing in Rowan."

"That's escalation all right," Smart said. "When does she start enforcing?"

"She starts patrol tomorrow. This is her last day at the Temple."

The Temple was a small cavern in which red and blue stalactites and stalagmites in fantastic shapes lined a volcanic tunnel that led to a platform of black lava that somehow resembled a table of sacrifice. Everyone from the Shoshone to the mountain men and early Mormons had regarded it with a certain dread. Standing as it did amid the three-square-mile tortured moonscape of black cinder lava, the tunnel, in its sacerdotal spookiness, seemed close to artificial. It was the centerpiece of the park and Rowan always concluded her ranger-guided walks there.

"I'll be damned," said the poet Smart. "Well, tell her I'm on my way, would you, John?"

"Sure will."

Not long after starting his drive, he felt cheated of everything the morning might have provided. A little interior clarity and light. Hope.

He had taken the first drink in Flagstaff, his second stop, a margarita before dinner when they had all gone out for the famous, fabulous Mexican food — he and the professors and the attractive woman librarian who had attended what they had been pleased to fatuously call his "craft lecture." He had taken the drink because he could see that the librarian was attracted to him, ready in fact to sleep with him that night if he should make the move. But he was afraid of not performing, of impotence.

He put the big lake behind him and took the interstate eastward, through Reno and into the desert. Trucks roared past him, the highway weariness oppressed. Brown peaks lurked on the edge of vision, a sad wind blew across the creosote plain. Smart tried to remember his poem. There was a part he could not recall, about predatoriness, the fish living in the sea as men do on land. At Winnemucca, he left the interstate and drove north.

Four hundred miles away, during her lunch break, Ranger Rowan Smart drove her khaki-colored state golf cart from the Temple to the trailer she shared with John Hears the Sun Come Up. John was at home doing a wash in the machine. Their trailer had no dryer; they used a clothesline, half concealed like the trailer itself behind a stand of lodgepole pines less than a mile from the monument headquarters. Rangers were paid minimum wage.

"Your father's coming tonight," John said when he heard Rowan come into the trailer. "He telephoned."

"I knew it was today," Rowan said. She was fair, freckled and blond, with a long plain pretty face. She had bright blue wizard's eyes as striking as her father's and her face was flushed. "Why didn't you call me at the Temple?"

"Figured you'd be home."

She went into the sleeping compartment and began to change her clothes. She was taking off the gray work slacks she wore at the Temple and replacing them with her military gray-striped breeches and the expensive English riding boots she had bought herself years before in Alexandria, Virginia.

"What you want for lunch?" John asked. "I went to Yamoto's. I got some pretty good tomatoes."

"No lunch," she said. She went to the mirror on the bathroom door in the sleeping room and inspected herself in the uniform of Smokey hat and ranger shirt and boots and trooper's breeches.

"You didn't eat breakfast. You on a fast or something?"

"I'm on a fast," she said. "I require a vision."

"I think you're doing crank, Rowan."

"What I need," she said, "is a drink." She came to the door of the sleeping compartment and they looked at each other. "Martinis, right? Look, John, I need you to go up to the state store and get us gin and vermouth. I need it for him."

"I'm working the gate this afternoon. I already got wine. I got steaks in case you want to make him dinner. Anyway," John said, "he says he's sober."

"Wrong," said Rowan. "Because if he were sober he wouldn't stop here. He'd give me a miss." She went back into the compartment and took another look at herself in the mirror. "Just like in the old days. Back to college. If he thought I could get him pot or coke, I'd see him. But if he was being Professor Straight and Narrow it was like hello goodbye Rowan, my dear. All right," she said, "wine'll do. I hope it's good, because he knows his wine."

"It's Georges Deboeuf red, the large size."

"That'll do," she said. She opened an aluminum drawer and took an envelope out and dipped her forefinger inside the flap and licked it.

"Let him be," John told her. "The past is past. I don't think he always remembers what happens on his trips."

"How can he not remember?" she asked.

"They're gonna get you, Ro," John said. "Peterson is gonna spring a random drug test on your ass. Anyone who knows you can tell when you're on crank. You figure to do it on mounted patrol?"

"No," Rowan said, chastened. "Never happen again."

Once, loaded, not on enforcement but on what they called at the monument "riding fence," she had ridden a cow pony half to death in a burst of romantic enthusiasm.

When she came out of the bedroom, John Hears the Sun Come Up looked at her in her boots and striped breeches.

"Put those on for him?"

"Who?" she asked. She was without any ability to conceal her intentions or schemes. "Who? Peterson?"

"Not Peterson," John said. "You know who."

"Yeah, I did," she said after a moment. "I did, so what? He likes them. He likes me to wear them."

"Well," John said, "you're thirty-one years old."

"Aw, shit," Rowan said sweetly, "you remembered."

By afternoon, Smart had gone far northward, though he was still among the dry lakes, salt flats and badlands. Soon he began to see aspen groves and chamisa and smell the sage. Presently there were red rocks and buffalo grass, piñon and juniper. He began to think of Rowan. She was his wildflower, outlaw, Girl of the Golden West. She had been born in Mendocino to a radical actually on the lam, a child of the old days. During the Patty Hearst affair, the FBI had hassled him about the whereabouts of Rowan's mother. But at that time he had not known where either of them were. He had been with his wife in Boston and his other, legitimate children, whose day-to-day adventures were his life then.

The FBI had been interested in him too, back then. His work had been so popular in the Soviet Union in those days. As a young man he had worked as a lumberman in forests not far to the west of his present road; Soviet publishing houses had always loved his poems about saws whipping back and sweat freezing in your hair, the crust of a frozen marsh collapsing underfoot, the absurdities of religion. And of course, in that era, the anti–Vietnam War poems. He was one of the American poets to whom the Soviet Writers' Union paid royalties, and he had often gone over there, and to Eastern Europe, to read. He had had many Russian women.

At last Smart crossed the first clear-running river, and he pulled off the road to go and stand beside it and listen to its tumbling run and smell the sage. Salmon?

> With Moby-Dick himself, they shared the Japan Ground
> And now under the sky of the Tanana, two thousand
>   miles from there, two hundred from the salt, in this
>   clear baptismal water, they're home
> To claim their lay, like the Nantucket whalers, their
>   fishers' portion.
> They make me feel like cheering.

Hearing the roar of a truck somewhere back along the two-lane road, bearish Smart, weeping for his lost poem, hurried in embarrassment back to his car.

Back up at park headquarters, across a small parking lot from the rail to the Temple, Rowan found the county sheriff, Max Peterson, waiting beside the glass counter of the bookshop. Phyllis Stowe, the sales clerk, had been minding the store. She and Peterson had been gossiping. They both stopped talking to watch Rowan as she came in.

"Here's my new police person," Peterson said to Phyllis with a wink. In his right hand he was holding a gun belt with a holstered pistol on it. He wore a big .357 in a silver-decorated

Mexican holster on his own belt. "She look tough enough to you?"

"She's mighty tough," Phyllis said, and seemed not to be joking.

"Come on, tiger," Sheriff Peterson said to Ranger Smart. He motioned her toward a small office off the headquarters lobby that said PRIVATE on the door. When they were both inside he closed the door. He was a huge man, six five, with massive shoulders and a bald shaven head to which he affected to apply wax. He had fierce curling mustaches which he waxed as well.

"Here you go," he said. He took the pistol from the belt he was holding and handed it to her, barrel toward the ceiling. "You gotta sign for it. And for the bullets."

Rowan took the pistol, swung it toward the closed window and sighted down the barrel, gripping it with both hands.

"Oh, wow," she said. "A .357! Heavy shit. Who can I shoot?"

"I can see," Peterson said, "where we got a lot of review ahead of us. I mean like a massive reorientation procedure has to accompany this assignment for you."

"Nonsense," Rowan said. "Absolutely not." She set about inserting the cartridges in the revolver's chambers. "I've done this before, Max, remember? I was an enforcement ranger for seven months in '94." She pointed the weapon double-handed toward the window again, pivoting so that it could cover the arc of the visible park outside. Peterson gently took the weapon back, handed her the belt and watched her buckle it on.

"First off, Rowan," Peterson said, "this here weapon is not a .357 Magnum."

"It's not?"

"Sorry about that. This here is a Colt Lawman. American-designed revolver, parts made in Spain or somewheres. Double action. Four-inch barrel."

"OK," she said.

"Now, Colt does a .357-caliber version of this and they do a .45-caliber, but what you have, what you will have here, is a plain old .38-caliber version. Six shots. Firing .38 slugs. With double action, you don't have to squeeze the trigger hard to cock it. You use your thumb."

"Well good for little me. But I can't stop a damn bear with this, can I? I can't stop a crack-crazed gangsta. So what good is it?"

"Very accurate weapon." Peterson watched her sign the form for the revolver. "You OK, Rowan? Everything all right?"

She gave him a quick affectionate glance with her striking blue eyes. He was at a disadvantage with Rowan Smart because, although he was a married Mormon and a bishop of the stake, he had been to bed with her.

"I mean, you attending your program? Everything like that?"

"What are you, Max, my parole officer? My confessor? My political commissar?"

"I hear your old man was a major Communist," he said. "That's what they say in town. Some ranchers say."

"Damn right," she said. "Mom was the same. Mom's buried in the Kremlin wall. I'm gonna be buried there too."

"The fact is, Rowan," Peterson sighed, "I'm worried about you. I wouldn't have put you on enforcement but it's not up to me."

"There you go," she said. "I don't work for you either."

Peterson flushed. "Now that's where you're wrong, sweetheart. Every law enforcement officer in this county works for me. And you, pal, you work under my direct personal supervision. You'll be subject to regular testing. I catch you stoned and armed, I swear I'll put you in the penitentiary."

"I'm clean, Max."

"Things are perverse," he said. "I got little Mormon farm

boys giving each other hand signs like they're Crips and Bloods. I'm up against it. I'm trying to protect the public. Do I have to protect them from you? Were you clean when you like to rode that quarter horse to death up by Sutler's Bar? I heard about that."

She frowned deeply, childishly.

"I told you, man, I'm clean."

Peterson fidgeted.

"You're the only officer we got around here with a Ph.D. That's supposed to mean you're smarter than the other guys. So don't go all dumb on me."

"I don't have a Ph.D.," she said. "I never finished my dissertation."

"Goddamn it, Rowan," Peterson said, "I don't give a good blip what you got. I need some law and order. I need this park not to be a hangout and I need you to help me. You know I like you," he told her. "I'm an easy guy to get on with. I just want you to be responsible."

"You are an easy guy, Max," she said. "When I first met you I thought you were one of the twelve Nephites who walk the earth."

He flushed further at her invocation of the Mormon tradition and then laughed. He had been to college and taken a sociology degree at a state university down in Utah and done a few years as a social worker in prison. He was a member of the Mutual Improvement Society and a scoutmaster.

"Just don't blow it, baby."

"Don't worry, Max."

As she started out, her .38 buckled on, Peterson closed the door she had opened. She looked at him puzzled.

"I don't know how to put this, Rowan. I mean, I don't want to embarrass you. You gonna wear those boots and britches on patrol? With your weapon?"

"I got mounted patrol tomorrow," she said. "Why not?"

He paused and then spoke slowly.

"I don't know how to put this."

"That's what you just said. What don't you know how to put, Max?"

"For . . . psychological reasons," he said, looking at the floor, "I don't think female law enforcement officers should wear provocative clothing. And I think you look good enough to . . . I think you look real nice in that rig. And with your gun belt, you know . . . you're kind of provocative."

"You mean I'm a leather trip, Max? Sort of S-and-M like."

"I mean I know how bad guys think. How men think. Makes me wonder what you got in your own mind. So there it is. I don't like you getting yourself up like that."

"It's standard service uniform."

"Oblige me, Rowan."

"Male bullshit," she said.

"Jeez, you called it. Not me."

"All right, all right," she said. "I'll see you around."

There was a stretch of road, a time of afternoon when he could see the great peaks to the west shining. As the sun declined toward them, they seemed to remove themselves from sight. As he drove, a sudden storm came out of the east. The piñon-dappled hills were higher now and fingers of lightning struck the taller trees and set them ablaze, blackening the trunks and the ground around them. But in a few minutes the storm was gone, except for the smell of ozone and pine smoke, and there was hardly any rain.

The road ascended by degrees, among ponderosa pine. A highway marker declared him to be entering Shoshone County, whose state university, still a hundred miles away, would be the site of his reading. The road approach to Shoshone County, which appeared to constitute a modest rise, was proclaimed by its marker to stand at seven thousand feet above sea level.

He swung round a turn and encountered an orange MEN WORKING sign. Just beyond it stood a young flagman, about college age. He had on a Day-Glo vest over a poncho and a yellow hard hat from which his long blond hair protruded.

"Five minutes," the boy said when Smart rolled his window down a crack. He kept staring at Smart, holding up a red hand-sign that said STOP, shielding his eyes from the restored sunlight.

"Are you William Smart?" he asked the poet finally.

"Bless you, son," said Smart. "Yes, that's me."

"They had your picture in the cafeteria yesterday." The young man kept on gawking stupidly. "I read your poem. We had to read one in class last year."

"Good for you. Which one?"

"Umm," said the young man. "Not sure."

"You don't remember it?"

"It went like . . . it had like fields in it. Like roads in it?"

"Right," Smart said. "I have a few like that." He was quite ready to see the funny side. "How appropriate, since we're on a road at this very moment. And there are fields out there." He cleared his throat to keep his temper. "Do you go to Shoshone?"

"They had your picture in the cafeteria yesterday," the youth said.

"Think it's still there?" Smart asked.

"Huh?" A distant siren had sounded. The youth reversed his sign so that it read SLOW. He seemed to be pondering an answer as Smart rolled up his window and drove on, passing workmen along the shoulders, their rollers and asphalt trucks.

A poem with fucking roads in it, Smart thought, cackling. A field in it! Of course they were little morons at Shoshone State, he reflected. But pretty kids, grandchildren of Mormon ranchers and Basques and Cornish miners. The cafeteria sold pasties. It was adorned with his picture that week because he was on his way to read there.

He turned the radio on and found himself within range of the college transmitter. There was a nice flute piece by Carl Philipp Emanuel Bach. When it was finished the announcer, who had apparently struggled in speech course to overcome some palatal impediment, declared, "Together we can make cystic fibrosis history." Smart turned it off.

But one couldn't blame the kids. The faculty were incompetent and corrupt. Enraged ex-nuns, paroled terrorists of the left and right, senile former state legislators. But to whom, he wondered, did he owe his own inclusion in the sacred syllabus? So that the very yokels at the crossroads were provided the exultation of forgetting his field and road poems.

And what, Smart wondered, would they do with their lives up there once they'd duly read and forgotten? Manage Kmarts? Incinerate nuclear waste? Clerk for the Fish and Game? Ranching was for millionaires now, the mines and forests were objects of speculation. But how beautiful it had once been, he thought, the morning light, the trout rising at dusk. It was his land, he had worked it, his people had gone west with handcarts on the Oregon Trail, though they had settled farther along, closer to the ocean. In his day, a lumberman, a miner, worked his heart out, proud of his body's strength, hating his bosses, loving his fellow workers, swearing by the union. The boys ten years older than Smart had gone into the war against Hitler. Smart had joined up, signed on with the navy when the judge required it, after he and his friends had been caught stealing Forest Service equipment. The alternative was the State School for Boys, an institution so dreaded and fearsome that only the meanest and craziest got themselves sent back. No Shoshone State to go to then, where regional poetry was learned and forgotten.

Passing an alder grove with his windows down, he was startled to catch for a moment the robotic bleating of a backhoe. The sound made him pull off the road.

The grove was deserted. The prairie wind carried a weight of silence and he realized suddenly that the sounds were those of a mockingbird. It must have listened for days to a road crew's machines and incorporated the backhoe into its repertoire.

It was impossible for him then not to poetize. And it was impossible for him not to think: How the Russians would have loved such a poem once. Nature and machine in literal harmony, labor and wilderness under the broad sky. The fact was that, these days, Smart was not nearly as welcome over there as he had once been. Time was, his appearances had filled hockey rinks; he had gone drinking with Yevtushenko. Perhaps they thought, the new bunch, that he had been a little tight with the old crowd, a little too accommodating of the cultural command, the official poetasters and their masters. He had seen it as working against the Cold War. He had never thought of his work as political; he had assumed people there had genuinely liked what he did and would continue to do so.

It even seemed that the end of the Cold War had undermined his status in the United States, his credentials as rebel. As though people were less interested as the dangers waned. Then he had had his campus problems. Harassment. Absurdity.

Back in the car, he thought for a while of the Bird and the Backhoe. Of course there was a poem there. But so Russian, so Soviet, so much uplift and muscularity. Was it really worth doing? Someone somewhere had said of Rilke that if he had cut his chin shaving in the morning he would have bled poetry. Smart had once secretly thought that was equally true of himself.

> They make me feel like cheering,
> These fish, mere fish, at the cost of such voyaging, such
>   heroism, such wild adventure
> Fulfilling a purpose that was never their own.
> The mighty merciless will that made Leviathan
> Made them, sent them to sea, willed them unending strife.

He supposed that was hardly Rilke. He might have made a middle-level Soviet poet or the equivalent of one. Or else, he thought, he might after all be better than that. Starting out, his model had been Thomas McGrath, another poet from his part of the country. And as for the salmon poem — if he could only bring it back, it might be improved, honed into something worthy of its conception, the wonderful moment that had inspired it. In any case, he thought, except for fragments it seemed to be gone. But the excitement of the recollected poem, what seemed to him its possibilities, stirred a swelling of angina pain in his breast.

> . . . in order that there be fish, that there be something
>   rather than nothing
> In the appointed place.
> To serve that inscrutable disposition,
> Welcome them home now, with carnivore cries
> Life's champions
> Let them teem and die.
> To survive and teem and die is glory.
> God's will be done.

It would probably, he thought, be well to take the God part out.

There had not been that many visitors to the monument that afternoon. Fewer than a dozen in all, enough to constitute two groups. They would pass through the gate to park headquarters and tickets from Phyllis Stowe and, if they chose to, they might file into the little auditorium to watch a film on western North America during the early Cenozoic Era and the formation of volcanic structures. Watching it, Rowan had to muster all the goodwill of which she was capable — a thoroughly boring film and not even specific to that particular site. At least three other parks with volcanic configurations to display used it.

During the second showing of the film, Rowan went into the ladies' room and took the envelope out of her breeches pocket and licked the icelike crystal from her fingers and put some on her gums. She made it to the auditorium just as the lights were coming on. She had a quick look around to see if there were any children in the house. She always liked to make sure that children saw the part about the fossil record, the Eocene plants that had been carbon dated back millions of years. Her readiness to point out the implications to youngsters occasionally involved her in controversies with God-fearing parents. Sometimes she found these disputations tiresome. At other times she could barely get enough of them. The park superintendent, Mr. Bondoc, the man who had just assigned her to enforcement, preferred her to overlook difficult points of science. Fundamentalists ought to enjoy the parks too, and often wrote letters to their legislators.

"Do you have any films emphasizing creationism?" a bearded paterfamilias with a beaten-down wife and half a dozen children had once asked her.

"At the moment, sir," Rowan had replied, "we lack the documentation. We have folks in the field though."

"And what are they doing?"

Taking a shit, she had dearly wanted to say, but she had been sober at the time.

"Many people believe that the Garden of Eden is where Reskoi, the sky spirit, created Rainbow Girl," Rowan had told the man. "And where would we be without Rainbow Girl, kids?" she asked his children. "Without Rainbow Girl we wouldn't have turkey every Thanksgiving. Or corn."

"We don't happen to believe in Rainbow Girl," the man had said.

"C'mon," she asked him, "on a day like this? Everybody believes in Rainbow Girl."

Fortunately for Rowan, the man's complaining letter to Mr. Bondoc, attempting to refute the doctrine of Rainbow Girl and containing sarcastic references to Her, had made him sound like a lunatic to that unimaginative official.

Conducting the five tourists through the lava bed, Rowan was at her most enthusiastic. From time to time she was afraid there might be some spittle running down the side of her mouth, but that was just her imagination. The men appreciated her dashing uniform and the women seemed not to mind. Glimpsing herself in the reflective glass of the park headquarters on the way to the field, it seemed to her she looked like Ella Raines in *Tall in the Saddle*. Queen of the Cowgirls, the big iron on her hip.

As usual, she explained to her group that the field through which she conducted them was a composite lava field of fluid mafic formation. It was mainly cinder and ash which gave it its grim and witchy appearance, although there were also examples of lapilli and even some brachiated granite of volcanic origin, among which, in season, wildflowers grew. A few of the wildflowers, she pointed out, were still in evidence, withered and mummified: Indian paintbrush, lupine, death camas.

A teenage girl, the youngest person in the group, wanted to know why it was called death camas.

"Because some say it used to grow over graves, honey. Along the trail. And others say because the flower looks a little like a skull."

The brachiated lava had other plants.

"Wintergreen," Rowan told them. "And phlox. And I like this one because it's called ranger's buttons." And, as always, that got her a titter, as though it were amusing. "So when I die," she said, "and they bury me here on the lone prairie, you'll see some death camas over me and some ranger's buttons."

Another, lesser, polite titter.

"And maybe a mountain ash," Rowan said. "Anyone guess why?"

No one did. Rowan showed them her name tag, on the side of her shirt opposite her gold badge, holding it out between her fingers.

"Because my name's Rowan. And back in the old country that's a tree with red berries you hear about in songs, and here in our country it's a related tree that's got red berries too and they call it the mountain ash." She looked around at the lunar landscape. "Except I don't think they can get one to grow out here. Even for me."

Some of her colleagues unkindly called her lectures "The Smarty Rowan Show" because instead of being about mafic fluid and volcanic rock, they often had a lot to do with Rowan Smart.

Finally she led them all into the volcanic tunnel that led to the Temple, past the polychrome stalagmites to the table of ash and cinder. Rowan had them spread out around the black chamber while she mounted a rise behind the table. Phyllis Stowe had locked up the park headquarters and come to the Temple to oversee Rowan's wrap-up. Things were running late and Phyllis was annoyed.

"Now this," Rowan told her charges, "is what they call the Temple. Can you all see why?"

Everyone nodded.

"It does look like a temple, doesn't it? In fact, some Latter-day Saints at first thought it might be a temple of the tribe of Zebulon come to America. But that proved not to be."

"Who built it?" a middle-aged man asked. Someone always seemed to ask that question. The place was so fantastical in its range of color and light that people resisted the idea of its natural formation. It was as though they had lost their faith in nature.

Once she had had a European visitor on the tour who plainly

refused to believe Rowan's insistence that the cavern was natural. It was America and the visitor had required inauthenticity and illusion. But there were a thousand caves in the same colors within a few hundred miles, all quite natural.

"Do you think if we had made it," Rowan had asked the visitor, "we'd only charge you a buck to get in?"

It had been back in the days when the Europeans had fallen in love with New York subway graffiti and brought spray-paint cans with them on rafting tours and harassed the Indians.

"No one built it," Rowan said. "God built it."

The crystal was catching up with Rowan. She remembered that her father was on the way and all it entailed. She began to think of the times he had left her weeping, of the stories he had started to tell her and then gone away, leaving them incomplete. Sometimes she would imagine endings for them, hoping one day to surprise him with his own tales, but he would never remember what she was talking about.

"Were there like human sacrifices here?" the teenager asked. Everyone murmured echoes to the question. Phyllis Stowe looked at her watch.

"Seems like that kind of place, doesn't it?" Rowan asked. A certain type of kid always asked that question, and this girl, gawky, tomboyish, innocently flirting with Rowan, was the type. "There might have been. Someone used the cavern for ceremonies. Before the modern Indians lived around here there were Caddoan-speaking people who practiced a kind of human sacrifice."

A special silence fell. Rowan held them with her bright eyes.

"They had a legend like the one about Abraham and Isaac. They believed that the sun couldn't move unless blood was shed. Sun couldn't move because he couldn't see. Nothing would grow. Children would not grow up. So sometimes captive boys or orphan girls from the Bear Clan were put on the stone and killed. The girls were the ones who had a dream where they died. They were killed when a certain star appeared in the morning, and the people called the killing Morning Star Ceremony. We don't know what the star was. Probably it was the planet Venus."

"Were they like tortured?" the teenager asked.

"They were never tortured," Rowan said. "They died very quickly with an arrow through the heart because they were important girls. They were the grandchildren of Sun through his sons and daughters the Bears, and Sun needed their eyes to see. When Sun saw their blood he ran through the sky. We cannot make our sun stand still," Rowan declared, "yet we can make him run. This is where the girls might have been killed. Here in the Temple."

"Whoa," said the teenager.

The ones like her, Rowan thought, strange things would be going through their heads about now. Outrage about the orphan girls. Unfamiliar urges involving death and sacrifice. At least that was how it had been for her, and that was how she imagined certain kids felt. She would have liked to take this one aside.

"And the Bears," Rowan said, "to conceal the blood, to fool the other animals and to fool the girls, spread black cornmeal all around. And that's why the ash is here, and the cinders, all that black world, the mafic fluid. The world around here." She raised a hand, checking the pulse in her forehead. Her face felt hot and dry. "Well," she told her public, "that's all we have time for. I hope you've enjoyed your visit to Temple Cavern as much as we've enjoyed having you."

And she *had* enjoyed having them. In her present frame of mind, she might have gone on for hours.

"Where the heck did you get that sacrifice bit?" Phyllis asked discreetly as the visitors filed out. "I sure never heard it before."

"It came as a revelation," Rowan told her. "I was reading Karl Bodmer. I mean spiritually it was pretty fucking sublime."

"Thanks but no thanks," said Phyllis. "Well, I guess you're the expert."

"Sure," said Rowan. "I'd do it."

"Well," said Phyllis, "you certainly had them eating out of your hand."

"Thanks. Sorry I kept you late."

"I guess it's all right," Phyllis said. "Good luck on enforcement tomorrow."

The turnoff for Temple State Monument was in a village called Deerdrum, thirty miles from the college town in which Smart was scheduled to read. Just before arriving in Deerdrum, the highway passed through the Shoshone reservation where Rowan's friend John Hears the Sun Come Up had spent his childhood. The reservation was scattered over a vast plain of sage and greasewood that stretched toward distant mountains. Here and there over the plain were clusters of beige rectangular buildings and khaki trailers. These were the clinics, schools and meeting halls, some enclosed within chain-link fences. Each cluster was equipped with a few government-issue street lights of the sort found around prisons or military bases. The lights were automated, geared to daylight, so that as the weather changed in the enormous sky overhead they would flash on and off in reaction to passing banks of clouds. Near the road was a square white wooden church, freshly painted, with a little bell tower trimmed in green and a gold-colored cross.

Deerdrum itself had changed since Smart had last seen it. Once its fortunes waxed and waned with molybdenum production and the molybdenite mine outside of town. Now there was still some mining, but tourism was coming in. The hot springs along Antelope Creek had been dammed. Artists and soothsayers had moved out from the expanding university, and one of the town's restored gingerbread brothels had become a bed-and-breakfast. There was a Days Inn and even a florist.

Smart would have much preferred to stay in town; it was a tight squeeze in the trailer with John and Rowan. On the other hand, she would be insulted and there would probably be drinking and it was a long dark way from the park back to Deerdrum. Just before the turnoff he stopped at a state store and bought two bottles of Rioja. Then he drove on and took the left that led west toward the lava beds.

He felt no excitement or anticipation as he approached the park, and this was a little surprising. On the way, in pursuit of his poem, he had managed to make himself forget the storms that raged about Rowan and the terrible energy between the two of them. Old regrets troubled him as he got farther from town and deeper into the volcanic desert around the Temple. A sense of excitement and dread. You do what you want in the end, he thought, forget what you need to forget. You follow your bliss, as the man said. More than anything he wanted another drink. One of the things he had almost forgotten was the pitiless loneliness of the place.

"Shit," Rowan said when John met her in the yard of the trailer, "he's not here yet?"

John looked up the highway and shrugged. "Not yet."

"I was really hoping he would be," she said and began to pace back and forth in the yard. A faded striped sunshade protected part of the trailer yard, and even though the hot weather was over they had not yet taken it down.

"You were hoping but you were scared, right?" John asked.

"For God's sake," she said after she had paced outside for a few minutes, "I need a drink. How much wine did you buy?"

"Two of them big bottles. That'll make one for each of you," he said, "because I guess you know I'm not having any."

"I'm gonna have some now."

"You know," John said, "could be hours before he gets here.

You start drinking now, you're like to be passed out by the time he shows up."

"Ah," she said, brushing past him toward the aluminum door, "that's where you're wrong. I'm spinning my wheels. I sort of ate into that crank."

In the kitchen, she took a bottle of the Georges Deboeuf out of a paper sack and commenced drawing the cork with a Swiss Army knife corkscrew. John watched from outside the open door.

"What did you do that for?"

"What did I do it for? Let's see. Because Max was on my case because he thought my pants were too tight. Because I had a brace of pilgrims to instruct. Two braces actually."

When she had opened the wine she took her guitar out of the broom closet, dusted it off with her uniform cuff and sat on a plastic kitchen chair to tune it.

"So you gave your park tours on crank?"

She put the instrument aside and poured some claret into a jaunty breakfast juice glass and sipped it delicately.

"Not for the first time, old sport."

"I know it," John said. He stepped up into the trailer, went past her to the sofa and sat down wearily. "I suppose you made up a lot of hoodoo about Indian people. The way you do."

"I don't make things up," she said. "I never make things up."

"I've heard you. I wonder your nose don't get long as Pinocchio's out there sometimes." He looked her up and down, lazy-eyed. "And Max is right about your pants."

"I haven't heard any complaints from the public. You complaining?"

"Not me. I think you look good."

"Good? How about beautiful."

"You're beautiful regardless," John said. "Don't hurt to be more modest. Your face is all red from that shit. And how about removing your weapon? Or are you going to have your supper that way?"

Rowan took a deep drink of wine and grimaced.

"Christ, it feels good though," she said. She turned to him on the sofa and put his hand on the buckle of her gun belt.

"You gonna give him speed?"

"Are you kidding? He's an old doper from the great age of dope. He could do half a kilo while other people were doing a gram."

John looked at the trailer deck for a moment, his fingers interlaced.

"I'm not comfortable," he said, "when you been drinking and doing drugs. You know that, don't you? When we're intimate and you been drinking . . ."

Rowan picked up the guitar and began to sing: "When we're intimate, and I've been drinking, I get to thinking . . ."

"Oh shut up," John said. "Don't be so smart."

"Smart's my name, baby. Smart's my nature."

"Maybe you've forgotten," John said, "you've got in real trouble on that crank. I've seen you crazier than all get-out."

Rowan nodded. "You can never tell how strong it is or what's in it," she agreed, and strummed a few chords. "I guess that's because it's made by the Hell's Angels and not the Red Cross."

John picked up the afternoon paper and leafed through it.

"I don't know, kid. I ain't gonna have a good time tonight. I should go see my mother." He put the paper aside and stood up. His younger brother was making trouble for the old lady, hanging with a gang. John's mother had a drinking problem of her own. "Anyway, I want to buy a lottery ticket in town."

"Oh God," Rowan said, sounding truly frightened, "he's coming! I think I see his car."

Her friend looked stoically straight ahead.

"You gotta forget, Rowan. You have to realize what drunks

are like. He won't remember you that way. If he does . . . it's not good."

"What do I care what citizens and pilgrims think?" she demanded of him. "You yourself told me you thought it was all right."

"Some Indian people think it's all right. If it's what the spirit world wants."

"Well, I happen to think it is."

"Well, I happen to think it isn't," John Hears the Sun Come Up said. "I think that crank will take your life someday."

"Jesus," Rowan said, "it's him."

"I ought to stay," he said. "But only if you let me." When he looked at her she was licking the crystal from her fingertips.

"I hope God helps you. You should ask him."

"I'll ask him to stay too."

"Rowan . . ."

She put her hands over her ears, still staring out at the road. "I'm not hearing you."

"Yes you are," he said. "You are."

Smart parked beside their cars at the end of the dirt road that led to the trailer. Hers was a Volvo from the mid-eighties. John's was a Dodge pickup, suggesting commercials from vanished Super Bowl Sundays, the Spirit of America. They had the Park Service cart parked there too.

There were sprouts and carrots still growing in their garden. The carrots, he remembered, sometimes came round as medallions, from the shallow layer of soil above the igneous rock, flattened out against it.

He walked up to the trailer and knocked on the door. He had promised John Hears the Sun Come Up a new poem. Maybe he would magically remember the salmon poem. He might remember it word for word, he thought. Suddenly he found himself wondering what exactly he had been feeling that night beside the Tanana. Whatever it was, that was the subject of the poem. If he could bring that back, the words might follow.

Rowan stood in the doorway looking down at him. When he'd last seen her she had been flabby with drink but now her face was lean and tanned, although of course she was older now and there were wrinkles radiating from the corners of her eyes. She was in her uniform, slim and sleek. Her face was red and her blue eyes looked a little unsound. Along with mounting excitement in his chest he felt a quickening of caution.

Their kiss was brief and distant and they avoided each other's eyes. John stood and shook hands with Smart. Then they sat in the center compartment of the trailer. Smart, as guest of honor, took the small gray sofa. Rowan and John sat in plastic armchairs. The rest of the space was occupied by cases full of Rowan's books. There were more books in an adjoining stage closet. She had even jammed a tiny desk into the space. Looking around the small room, he saw a couple of yellow pads with what looked like verse in his daughter's handwriting.

"Writing poetry?"

She laughed self-consciously without answering.

"I'll have to read it," he said, "or get you to read it to me."

"She's a good poet," John said. He was drinking Sprite, staying with the program. Smart and his daughter drank the red wine. "Not as good as you," he said to Smart, "but pretty good."

"John's a connoisseur of poetry," Rowan said. "He's real diplomatic too."

"I know she's a good poet," Smart said. "She always has been. Since she was a little girl."

"We see the world through the same eyes," Rowan said. "That's literally true. Our eyes are the same. I mean look at them."

Both the men in the room found somewhere else to look.

"Do you remember any of my poems?" Rowan asked her father. "Do you remember the ones I used to send you from California? Maybe you never got them."

Smart had a recollection of his daughter sending him poems she had written. He had inscribed a book of his poems to her and she had made a folder of her poems and sent them to him. Then later, in college, she had published some poems in university literary magazines and sent them to him. He had never, as far as he could remember, responded.

"I do remember some of them," he said.

"Do you remember the one I wrote about the wind in the desert?"

"The one where you held the wind in your hands?"

Rowan put her glass down and raised both hands to her face. "Oh God! You remembered it!"

It was the one single poem of hers he remembered. She had written it after her mother had moved her to the women's collective in New Mexico. It was about ending up with nothing, with no one.

"Sure I remember it," Smart said, draining his glass. "I think I used it."

"Oh God," Rowan said. "I'm glad you did."

"How about playing for me?" Smart said. "Still got your pawnshop guitar?"

"Hey, I thought you'd never ask."

She played him an old Scottishy song he liked about the Rose and the Linsey-O and then a song she had written, from one of her poems. But he seemed not to notice it was her poem.

"Hey, what about that steak?" John said. "We gonna eat or what?"

"Sure," Rowan said without enthusiasm. Her eyes were fixed on her father. "I'll do it."

"No, no," Smart declared. He struggled up from the sofa and poured another juice glass of wine for Rowan and himself. "I'm cooking. I see mushrooms and your homegrown jalapeños. I'm the steakmaster.

"You know," he told them as he blundered about the kitchen, "I got thrown out of one of the casinos down on the lake. For being drunk, I guess."

"'Cause you look like a rodeo clown," Rowan said. She plunked a chord on the guitar and put it aside. "That's why."

John gave her a disapproving look.

"They seemed so goddamn angry," Smart said. "Like they hated me."

"Probably did," she said. She got up and went to the trailer lavatory. While she was in it John came up to Smart, one eye on the door. His voice was naturally so soft that it was always hard for Smart to hear him, and he was keeping it low.

"She's doing crank, Will. She's been doing it all day and I thought I better tell you."

"She seems in good spirits."

"That can change real fast. And she won't sleep and she won't shut up. So I hope you're ready."

"Actually," Smart said, "I'm really not."

"Then you shouldn't have come."

"You mean because I'm drinking?"

"You know what I mean," John said. He had been speaking with his eyes closed, as some Northwest Indians do when they are moved to show respect. "I love hearing your poetry, Will. But I'm not gonna stay and protect either of you. Not with the two of you like this."

With John's eyes closed to him, Smart drank the glass of wine down. His third.

"Your poetry's all you have," John Hears the Sun Come Up told Smart. This time he looked him in the eye. His own eyes looked flat, utterly unfeeling. "It's your soul, a good soul."

"Thanks," said Smart, touched.

"But you shouldn't go near her. Not now."

He went out without waiting for a reply.

When Rowan came out of the lavatory, they listened to his pickup roar to a start. He gunned the motor, braked hard backing out and took off explosively toward the highway.

"I'm glad he went." Her face was brighter. She looked around for where she had left her wine glass. "He's jealous."

"Jealous."

"Yes, he should be . . . I'd be if I was him."

"Will he come back?"

She gave Smart a dark crazy smile and shook her head. "Not tonight."

He watched her stand up and put a tape in her Sharp 4 recorder. It was Vivaldi, *L'Estro Armonico*. He saw that she was wearing a gun belt with a holstered pistol. The little space she stood in was piled from deck to overhead with books: *The Golden Age of American Anthropology*, Lewis Henry Morgan on the Iroquois longhouse, George Caitlin prints. There was also shelf after shelf on religion: the Gnostic Gospels, the works of Hans Jonas, kabbala, witchcraft, Wicca.

"Look at all your books, kid. You're still beguiled by magic."

"My books?" She laughed. Instead of sitting down, she stood beside his chair while the Vivaldi played. "You know when I was in high school the local cops flagged all the library books on witchcraft? They pulled me in. They thought my boyfriend was castrating cattle. Or I was. They told me I had to spy on the witches' coven in the high school or they'd send me to juvenile jail."

"Were you a witch?"

"I was a little bookworm. Writing my poetry. There wasn't even a coven." She laughed again. "You know, I tried to start one but I got bored."

Now he laughed and put a hand on her hip and patted it.

"You like the way I look, Will?"

"You look very . . . constabulary. I mean, what with the gun."

"They put me on enforcement. Can you imagine? I know more about the Temple, about the Paiute and Shoshone traditions, than any white-eyes in the state. So I'm supposed to chase over hill and dale after some dummy poaching 'lope. A bitch, right?" She licked her lips and offered him a soiled envelope. There was a crystalline powder at the bottom of it. "Want some? It's the famous ice. Crystal meth."

"No thanks."

"Go ahead," she said, moving closer to him, pouting slightly. "Because you know we'll get crocked and you'll go to sleep on me and how often do I get to see you?"

"I know what you mean."

"Go ahead."

He dipped his finger into the stuff so there was a small mound on his fingertip and licked it off.

"Easy," she said. "this is strong. You'll get shot out of a cannon."

"Right," said Smart. The drug seemed to kick in almost immediately. "I guess I can tell you this," he said. "I guess you're a pal."

"You can tell me everything, Will."

His heart raced.

"You know, I came unstuck on my last reading tour. I have to get my act together."

"How did you come unstuck?"

"I found myself in an office full of my poems. A professor's office. He had every volume I ever published. So I filled my briefcase with them, all my books, and I swung the case against his window. His office was in this ghastly brick tower." It seemed to Smart that he was speaking faster and faster. "I was trying to break the window, see. I wanted to break his window with my books."

"Were you drunk?"

"Of course I was drunk."

"Did you want to jump?"

"Yes, I suppose. But I could only shatter the inner layers of the window. I got his office full of glass and blood. It was after the harassment thing back east. And that was the end of my reading."

He stood up, dizzy again. The altitude, the drug. He poured himself another glass of plonk.

"But you oughtn't to die. You have work to do."

"Maybe."

"I think you're a great poet. Even my mother does."

"Does she?"

"She sure does. And all her friends."

Rowan's mother still lived on the commune in Mendocino. It was the place where, among flowers and flutes and midwifery, Rowan had been born. Rowan had spent a lot of her childhood there and Smart had seen very little of her.

"I had a poem for you, Rowan. I've been trying to remember it since I got west." He took another sip of wine to slow the rush of his heart.

"Oh, you have to," she said. "Take a little more crystal."

"You minx!" he said. "You've poisoned me."

"I'm not a minx. Or a mink or a weasel," Rowan said. "I want my poem."

"Once I spent years trying to remember a poem," Smart told her. "Twenty years maybe." He had seen the low range of mountains on the horizon through the little kitchen window and it was as though he were looking for his other lost poem out there. "It was a poem I wrote about a plane loaded with American salesmen breaking up over Mount Fuji. They'd won a selling contest, a free trip to the Orient. So they ended up falling down on Mount Fuji with their wives and their wallets and their Kodaks. Buddhist monks gathered up their bodies. I thought that was so amazing. But I lost the poem I wrote and I never could bring the sucker back."

"Sure," Rowan said. "Your Fall of Capitalism poem. I don't want that one. I want the one you wrote for me."

"God," Smart said, "if I sit down I'll never be able to stand up. How can you take that stuff?"

"Please," she said, "try and remember. It's important to me."

"Rowan," Smart said, "why don't I cook for us? We're letting good beef go to waste."

"How can you be hungry?" she demanded. "I don't want to eat."

"Well," he said, "maybe I'm not. But we should eat or we'll get plastered."

As though she were spiting him, Rowan finished the wine in her glass and poured more for both of them.

"I'll make you remember," she said. "I'll make you remember me. Then you'll remember my poem."

She went up to him then and took his hand and kissed it. He put it against her flushed cheek and brushed her straight blond hair.

"My *fanciulla del west*," he said. He looked away from her at the sad greasewood landscape outside. "My cowgirl. My Rowan tree."

When he sat down breathless on the sofa she nestled beside him.

"I was in Alaska, Rowan. Must have been twenty-five years ago. You were little. I saw these salmon going up the Tanana to spawn. I thought it was so moving."

"I can see you standing there. Like a big bear."

He began to cry. "Sorry, kid. I'm coming apart again, I guess."

She put her arm under his and put his hand on her thigh and stroked it for a moment.

"Don't you see," she asked, "how our eyes are just the same?"

"Yeah. Well, see me standing there. In that white night."
With his hand still on her thigh, he leaned his head against the
back edge of the sofa and looked at the fake wood panels on the
trailer ceiling and tried to recite the poem:

> Like elephants, swaying
> Straining with the labor of each undulation,
> They labor home.
> The river is forever swift and young,
> Forever renewed, beyond history . . .

He worked to catch his breath and had another swallow of
wine.

> But these, elephant-eyed
> Under the skirl and whirl and screech of gulls
> And swoop of eagles,
> Are creatures of time's wheel.
> Under the pale ultra-planetary sky of the white night
> I feel for them such love
> And, for their cold struggle, such admiration
> In my overheated heart.

"I can't, baby," he said finally. "Anyway, I don't think it's very
good."

"Such love," she repeated.

"I don't know what it was about," he said. "I admired these
fish. Being finished, coming home. They had done what they
were meant to do. Whereas I never had." He closed his eyes and
put a hand on his chest, under which his heart was racing. "Or
maybe it was just about the moment. I don't know."

"Such love," she said.

"When whatever happened between you and me, Rowan . . .
What shouldn't have, what I shouldn't have let happen. I was
on that tour. I had come apart."

"I see," she said.

"And I wanted some comfort and love. I wanted it so much."
He was weeping. He wiped his nose, bearlike.

"And do you now?"

"Yes I do."

She stood in front of him and took his hands and folded them
behind her back. He withdrew them quickly. Rowan tensed and
pursed her lips. Her anger frightened him.

"The poem is about us," she said. When he tried to speak, she
interrupted him. "Yes it is, it's about us."

He realized that she was trying to kiss him on the mouth.

"This is just drugs," Smart said. He stood up, trying to escape. It was like a dream, suggesting something that had happened once before in another world. "John will be back. What
will he think of you?"

She laughed and pushed herself against him, standing on tip-
toes in her boots, pressing her face into his.

"John will not be back, Will. John is a Wind River Shoshone
and his attitude is from that culture and believe me it's peculiar
to that culture. Besides, he's a passive-aggressive."

Smart collapsed back on the miniature sofa. She kept trying
to kiss him, fondling him, at his belt, his clothes.

"Rowan," he said, "my sweet. I'm lonely. I wanted to see
you."

"But you don't want me."

"Oh yes," Smart said, "I want you. I want all the things we
didn't have. I do. But I can't make them happen, can I?"

"But you don't want me," she said.

"Listen," he said, "you were just a pretty girl."

"Then we shouldn't have done it before, should we?" Rowan
said. She fixed him with the mirror of his eyes. "Then you never
should have done it and I never should have gone for it. But I
did. You're the only one I want. Ever since then. All my life
maybe."

"I was drunk," Smart pleaded. "I was on drugs. I was certifiable. I took some comfort. I was desperate."

"Then," she said, "what about me?"

"We fucked up, baby. It happens."

She turned on him with such violence that he jumped. She was a big girl, strong as he had been, only an inch or so shorter than his six two. She resembled him so much.

"You like me like this. I know you do. I've been waiting for you all day."

"God," he said. "You're still a child, aren't you?"

He put out his hands and took her by hers and sat her down beside him.

"This is how it was, baby. I hardly knew you. It was as though you weren't my daughter." It was hard to face her grieving, crazy eyes. "You were the most gorgeous creature I had ever seen." He laughed, against his will. "You were so adoring. I couldn't help it." He tried to embrace her but she avoided his embrace.

"I'm the only one of your children," she said, "who has your eyes. We're the same."

"Just a beautiful young girl," Smart was saying. And after a fashion he remembered or thought he remembered how it might have happened. As beautiful a young girl as he had ever seen. So young and gorgeous and besotted with him. What a fool he must have been, a weak, self-indulgent drunk. In those days, when he had let it happen, when he had done it, he had thought he could do no wrong. He had actually complained to friends of being made too much of. God knew what they had secretly thought of that, of him. As if no bills would ever be charged to his account.

The drug was driving the rhythms of his heart and brain to a pitch he could not manage.

"Your poem," Rowan said, "it's about me. It's about you coming back to me. Us both coming back where we belong.

Which is together. Always," she said. "Always because we have the same flesh, we have the same mind, the same eyes."

Smart caught his breath. "You've taken that drug," he said.

"We see the same things at the same time. I know your poems as well as you do."

He got to his feet and tried to shake off the tremors that assailed him.

"I'll tell you what," Smart said. "I've got through many a night on many a drug. I'll sing to you like I used to. Sometimes, anyway. We can read poems to each other. Then it'll be morning, see. We'll hear the birds. The sun'll be up. The drug will be over. We'll have survived."

Without looking at him, she walked into the darkness at the sleeping end of the trailer. Finding himself alone, he went back to the kitchen and drank more wine. He had made a mistake, another one. Another old bill presented. No end to it. He curled up on the sofa with the light on. There was only darkness and silence at the far end of the trailer where his daughter lay.

After a while, he began passing out, lapsing into a shallow sleep from which the methedrine kept waking him. In each space of sleep, a pool of uneasy dreams awaited him. From each he kept rising against his will, finding himself thirsty and breathless in the harshly lit trailer. Once he dreamed of the salmon. In the dream it seemed to him that he could remember it all, verse by verse, in Rowan's voice:

> Fighting their way on up the Tanana
> Two hundred miles now from the sea
> And when I try to see their eyes,
> What I see, under the flow,
> Are old elephants' eyes
> Appearing wise but still
> No wiser than Creation.

Her warm cheek was against his temple and she was reciting:

> All their long years they saw the predators fail,
> All the same time their own predations fed them.
> What a life, the life of the roving sea!
> Where fish live, the poet said,
> As men do on land.

Her voice was so sweet and he loved her so much. He was himself accounted a good reader. Then it occurred to him that he had never rendered those lines for her. It was a part of the poem he had forgotten. Before he could open his eyes to inquire, the bullet struck his brains out.

She did not holster the weapon but held it hot against her left hand. After the noise, the deaf-and-dumb horror, the vitriol of her grief welled up to every part of her where it could curl and pool. Even through the wine and the drug she felt it burn. For nearly an hour, until the crystal energy failed, she pressed her wine- and speed-stained maw against his red mouth, trying to breathe life back into the mess she had made of him.

"Sorry, Daddy," she said. "Sorry, Bear."

She had not been able to get him through the night. Nor he her.

Rage. But she had not wanted him dead, not at all. Only to have something. Something, anything, between childhood and death.

All night long she sat facing the ugliness she had worked. His pants were undone. Dreadful. Had she done that? Maybe, pursuing the salt of her own generation. Trying to get home. She must be in some confusion, she thought, about which coupling had created her.

Both, she thought. She was Rowan, the creature of both those lyings-down. Under the mountains, on sweet grass, among the musky ash and laurel. Name it and claim it. She could no longer remember the moment of killing. So he forgot he fucked me, she thought. And I forgot I shot him. Sorry about that, Bear.

She had destroyed his eyes. She must not do it twice. She owed him that.

There seemed some necessity to wait for dawn, out of love or respect or fear of the dark. When she could no longer drink, she kept plastering her face with crystal. That way her mind might become entombed in it, like one of those captives of the plains they candied with honey and earth and roasted, and there remained hardly a man but only a bear-shaped thing, eyeless, mouthless, blazing away, blackening like pottery, burning alive in a glazed silence. Crystal could do it.

When she went out of the trailer, the sky was growing light. Somewhere out on the flats she heard the cough of a coyote. And overhead Venus was at its western elongation. Phosphorus, Lucifer, the Morning Star.

On her way to the Temple, she holstered the revolver she had cradled all night long. She carried the wine bottle in her left hand; the envelope of crystal was in her uniform breast pocket. At the door of the Temple she paused to look at the pure early morning. Moment by moment, it was beautiful. Things could only be beautiful that way.

She let herself into the Temple and walked past the columns, licking the last of the speed from the envelope, washing it down with wine. It made her impatient to be gone. When she came to the stone of sacrifice she stood beside it. She had brought the Caddoans, the Pawnee maidens, clear across the plains from Nebraska to die on it. All in her imagination, and that of the pilgrim children to whom she told the story. But real Pawnee maidens had died under the Morning Star, as she would. For a while she thought of lying down on the stone and doing it and being found that way.

But I'm only the dead poet's speed freak bastard daughter, she thought. She went into the little utility room beside the cavern entrance and pulled free the yellow felt marker that was held fast to the door by a piece of string. There was a public bathroom next door, and she went in and relieved herself so that things would be as clean as they could be. Then she washed her hands and dropped the wine and her empty envelope of speed into the trash can along with the paper towel.

She sat down beside the trash can with the revolver beside her on the tile floor and felt along her chest for her heartbeat. She was EMS-qualified. If she stretched her arms up and leaned her head back, it would part her ribs a little, which might make it easier. When she was satisfied she had found her heart, she held the cloth of her uniform shirt taut and marked a cross over it with the marker.

Let them anatomize Rowan, she thought. Not on the stone of sacrifice, thanks, just up against the shithouse wall. But she wouldn't hurt his eyes again, not blind the bear again.

Sitting propped up against the cold wall, she leaned her head back and raised her left arm in the air as far as it would stretch, fingers extended. She put the barrel of the Lawman against the X on her chest and said her own name and her father's and pulled the trigger.

Max Peterson came out around six-thirty, alone, as soon as John Hears the Sun Come Up called him. John had called him at home instead of through the dispatcher. Together they walked over the grounds, from the trailer to the Temple.

"I don't suppose you killed them, did you, John?"

"Nope," John said.

They were standing in the ladies' room where dead Rowan sat, her father's eyes preserved in blank surprise, slowly losing their luster. Peterson punched the swinging hinge of the covered trash can, where they had found the envelope.

"That fucking pervert Communist son of a bitch. It was his fault. *He* fucking killed *her.* That's the way it really went."

"Fuck" was a word Peterson rarely used.

"It was the speed," John said. "It always made her crazy. She was a little crazy anyway."

"He probably brought it."

"No, she had it."

"Well, what the hell did you let her have it for?"

"If I'd 've found it," John said, "I'd have got rid of it. She had it at work. Then I couldn't take it off her, short of tying her up."

"You should have tried."

"Maybe," John said.

They walked back to the trailer and stood over Smart's body and Peterson looked down at what was left of him.

"Goddamn him, the filthy bastard," Peterson said.

"Well," John said, "she loved him."

Peterson stared at John Hears the Sun Come Up as though he had taken leave of his senses.

"He was her *father,* for Christ's sake. The scumbag."

"He wasn't a bad guy," John said. "He was a good poet."

"What the hell is your problem?" Peterson shouted. "Every goddamn thing I say you gotta contradict it? The fucking man was her *father,* John. The relationship was perverted. Who the hell cares about good poet or such shit?"

"He wrote a poem about salmon I liked," John said.

Peterson sighed. "You're a crazy Indian son of a bitch, John. I'm truly impatient with you." He looked around the trailer a last time. "Jeez, she had every kind of queer satanic book. He bring her up that way?"

"I don't know," John said. "I guess." There was no point in making Peterson angrier.

Peterson went out to his car to call the dispatcher's office.

Presently the park people would be coming out and the photographers and twelve kinds of cop and probably the press and even television.

Smart's poem about the salmon had been folded away in Rowan's *Dictionary of Classical Mythology*, and a few pages beyond it was another poem, about a bunch of American tourists falling out of the sky on a Japanese mountain. John Hears the Sun Come Up particularly liked the one about the salmon. It made him able to see very clearly the fish and the buffalo and the place Smart was writing about. It reminded him a little of Robert Frost, his favorite white poet.

He went outside and watched the dawn swell over the low mountains to the east. He thought he would sell the trailer but keep her books. It was not that he needed them for her memory — he could take care of that — but they were good books and interesting. As for the rest, there was no point in keeping any of it. People disappeared. There, in the country of the Ghost Dance, people disappeared and their songs with them. They became ghosts and their songs ghost songs. Teenagers in the Indian high school got drunk and died, disappeared forever, knowing hardly anything to sustain them in the ghost world.

The powder, the crystal, was death; as soon as he had seen it shining on her finger, glistening with that death glow it had, under her nose, bringing the heart's blood to her cheeks, he had known the two of them would die. Smart the poet would go to the place he had seen the salmon; people passing through might find his ghost there and hear his songs.

"Will?" he asked the silence. "Mr. Smart?" He had Smart's manuscript in front of him. He read the first line of Smart's salmon song.

"Like elephants, swaying."

He might try singing it one day. Singing it in the Shoshone-Paiute language. No word for elephant, just say "elephant."

"Rowan?"

Her, she would be out in the greasewood with the thousand poems she knew, her songs and all the stories she made up. Well set up out there in the ghost world. People alone would hear her songs and be afraid. Her eyes would, like her father's, look out from lost blue places. High lakes at certain times of afternoon, the evening sky, the cornflower, the shad violet. Easy to bring her ghost back — burn a little sweet grass, fix her guitar maybe and play it, she would come. Her and her father, called Smart, all their songs, two poets.

CPSIA information can be obtained at www.ICGtesting.com
Printed in the USA
240593LV00001B/146/P